UPHEAVAL

UPHEAVAL

RYAN J SLATTERY

ISBN- 13: 978-1517793944
ISBN- 10: 1517793947

Cover design by Ryan Slattery and Josh Eaker.

www.rjslattery.com
@RJSlatts on Twitter
RJSlattery on Instagram

For Clare Slattery
May your life be full of adventure

TABLE OF CONTENTS

TABLE OF CONTENTS

Delver's Map
(subject to continual change)

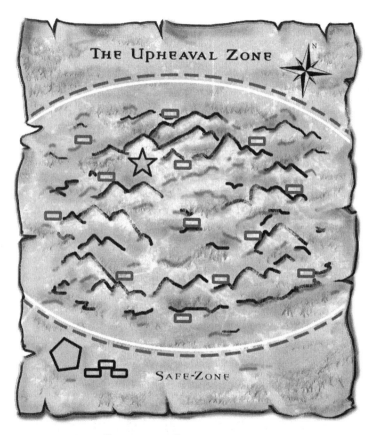

The Upheaval Zone

N

Safe-Zone

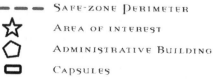

- - - - - Safe-zone Perimeter

☆ Area of interest

⬠ Administrative Building

▢ Capsules

Chapter 1

Interrogation Game

The bad news? I forged my parents' signatures on official government paperwork. The good news? No one seemed to know.

Nevertheless, I sat in the office of a government official in a brown suit. He sifted through papers in a manila folder with my name printed on the outside—Gage Ward.

"You know what you're getting into is dangerous, don't you, Gage?" he asked, looking up from his papers.

He peered at me over his thin reading glasses. My arm twitched on my leg. Did he figure out that I'd forged the papers after all?

"What do you mean, sir?" I asked.

"Delving for objects after an Upheaval is treacherous; there are many dangers."

"Of course I know that," I said. "I signed the paperwork just like my parents did."

He closed the file and laid it on his desk. "A fourteen-year-old's signature isn't legally binding. You know some people think the Upheavals will destroy the world. What would you do if that happened?"

Normally, if someone said that to me, I might've laughed. But a lot has happened in the last five years. In 2011,

Upheavals, huge earthquakes, started shaking the earth to its core. But more importantly, they'd revealed that there was intelligent life on earth long before us humans got here. Actually, those who were here first were far more intelligent.

But there are those who think that the Upheavals are going to destroy the world, which is probably why the man in the brown suit asked me that question.

I would've been worried, but I'm sure he asks that question to all the new recruits. And answering it right could fast-track me to a good excavation site. There were probably plenty of candidates like me who would answer that question terribly.

But I know, and Mr. Brown-suit knows, that to get anywhere in life, you have to play the game, and there's no better puzzle solver in the world than me. That's why I said:

"Easy, I'd save the world."

Mr. Brown-suit's eyebrows dropped and he tilted his head. Obviously, I'd hit that one out of the park and left him dumbfounded.

He folded his arms. "Okay Gage, how exactly would you do that?"

"It's all cause and effect," I said. "Make the wrong move, and the world dies. It's just a matter of finding the right move. Like chess. At any point there are tons of bad moves that will make you lose. I just happen to always play the best move."

Mr. Brown-suit shook his head. The analogy must've gone right over his head. I should've known, too. He works a desk job. He's got Sudokus all over his desk, and none of them are even close to right. He's not exactly the Einstein of his field.

He opened a drawer and sifted through some more file folders and pulled a paper right up to his face. "Speaking of chess, this says you have great aptitude for creative problem solving."

I nodded. "Sure, I'm great at all kinds of puzzles. If you want I can help you out on this Sudoku here. You're actually really close on this one."

He pulled the paper down and squinted at me. "No thanks," he said through his teeth. He opened another drawer and pulled out a Rubik's cube. "I wonder if you could solve this cube using the Singmaster Method." He handed it to me.

"Timed?" I asked.

"You have five minutes."

I stifled a laugh. I'd have more trouble counting my fingers if they were labeled one-to-ten. The Singmaster Method was for amateurs—solving the cube one side at a time. Maybe other recruits had trouble with that kind of thing, but not me. I wanted to get to the best excavation site, so I wasn't about to do amateur work.

My hands whizzed that cube so fast I doubt Mr. Brown-suit could even see it. Of course I used the optimized Waterman method, solving it altogether instead of one-side-at-a-time.

"Time," I said, holding out the completed cube.

"Under a minute," he said, nodding. "Impressive, Gage." He wrote a small message on my file, then stood up and left the room. He must've been so impressed he'd gone to consult with someone.

After a while, the ticking of the clock started to bore me out of my mind. The walls were all eggshell white and undecorated. I finished one of his Sudokus to pass the time. I know he didn't want me to, but he'd thank me later.

Finally he returned. No one was with him and he didn't say a word about why he left. He sat back down, looked at his folders and continued the interview like nothing happened.

"Your knack for spatial comprehension is very important when you're dealing with Upheavals. That's what really got our attention on your tests."

Spatial Comprehension? I guess he meant that I could see moves ahead in three-dimensional puzzles, like the Rubik's cube. But it was something else he said that confused me.

"What test? I didn't know I was being tested."

"Everyone's tested. It's all in those boring fill-in the blank standardized tests at school. Why do you think we chose to interview you in the first place?"

"I thought those were just for the State."

He laughed. "Most of it is, but we've added a few questions that only matter to us. It's a new world now, and we need the best minds to find the best technologies."

Normally I wouldn't have minded the compliment, but I hated being tested without knowing it. It's not a fair game when one of the players doesn't even know he's supposed to be playing. Still, it was a good thing I didn't do what most people did and fill in random circles.

"So, what happens now?" I asked.

"You'll leave home. We fly you out to one of our camps, and we see if you can handle the pressure. Are you in?"

That's when I made the worst decision of my life.

Chapter 2

The Not-so-Safe Zone

They gave me a sealed envelope when the helicopter landed. "Top Secret" was stamped across it in large red letters and "Dr. Renner" was the name printed on it.

And it wasn't just the envelope that was top secret, either; they kept *everything* secret here. I wasn't even allowed to tell my parents where I was going. I wouldn't want to tell them anyway. That was the best part about it, actually. For the first time, they weren't in control of what I did with my time.

I did want to tell my friends though, but I wasn't allowed to do that either. First of all, we weren't allowed to use cell phones. Something about interference in the Upheaval-zones that made them inactive. But more importantly, *I* didn't even know where I was going.

Did I mention they kept everything secret?

The helicopter ride was awful. Mr. Brown-suit said that I'd have a guide to answer all my questions on the ride in, but I'd ask a question and Mr. Russell just ignored me. He had a head-set on, which made me think he was in constant contact with important people, but he was probably just listening to music. I bet he was into Country. His skin was tanned and he was big as a tractor, with more fat than muscle. I think he was raised in a barn somewhere in Iowa or something. He had this gap in his teeth, which I normally wouldn't notice, but he breathed with his mouth wide open.

"Here's you safety manual," Mr. Russell said, shoving a rather thick book at me.

I weighed the tome in my hand. It was kind of rude, but honestly, I was quite relieved the guy could move his mouth.

"So I'm supposed to have this read by…"

Mr. Russell just shook his head, mouth wide open.

The pilot's voice came from behind me. "We'll be landing in about five minutes. Has Russell given you the rundown of what to expect?"

Mr. Russell smiled. I could tell because teeth appeared in his stupid open mouth.

I turned to the pilot on the other side of the wall. "He hasn't told me anything. Is he supposed to be telling me something?"

"He hasn't told you anything? Russell, why do you do this every time we come to this location?"

"What's it matter?" Mr. Russell asked. "They'll be closing this dump down any day now. I don't know why they'd choose a little shrimp for this kind of work anyway. They're just wasting his time and ours."

Typical grownup. Always determining what is and is not a waste of time for *my* life.

"The only one wasting my time is you," I said. "Just do your job and tell me what I need to know."

It was hard to hear through the *chop-chop-chop* of the helicopter blades, but I was pretty sure I heard the pilot chuckle when I confronted Mr. Russell.

His mouth closed and his face scrunched like he was picking a nasty booger. "It's all in the book, kid."

"The name's Gage. And when exactly should I have this book read by?"

"One minute 'til we reach the Junkyard," the pilot said.

The area below came into view and I figured out why they called it the "Junkyard." The terrain was a labyrinth of earth. Spires of rock jutting out here and there, plenty of craters and caverns—just the place you'd want to spend months exploring for ancient technology.

Mr. Russell tapped the book in my hands. "It'd be good to have it read before we land."

What a jerk. I gripped the book so tightly my fingers turned white. That way my hands wouldn't accidently slip and clasp onto Mr. Russell's neck.

After landing and departing, the pilot put his hand on my shoulder. He was older than I'd expected. Mr. Russell was probably thirty; the pilot was double that.

"Sorry about Russell. If you know only one thing, it's that you need to find shelter if an Upheaval starts. Find a capsule. You'll be safe in one until it's over. Best of luck to you, son."

He handed me the sealed envelope for Dr. Renner and pointed me into the maze of stone skyscrapers made from the Upheavals.

But it wasn't all natural terrain; there were also some manmade structures. And when you're dealing with Upheavals, you go for more practical structures—something that can withstand the earth cleaving in half and jutting up and down.

There were a number of egg-shaped rooms, a little larger than a truck. Those were the capsules.

But what really caught my eye was a girl with blond hair climbing through the rubble, apparently alone.

Before I could ask the pilot about her, the helicopter'd already left me alone to find my way to Dr. Renner's office. Luckily, jerk though he was, Mr. Russell had supplied me with a map. The good news was there was a "safe-zone" perimeter around the Upheaval area for dorms and an administration building where Dr. Renner's office would be. The bad news was that I never made it there.

I hadn't taken but two steps when it happened. A siren blared in the air. Before I knew what was going on, the earth started to rumble and I heard a distant scream. My heart pounded in my chest.

This was bad! It had to be that girl I'd seen earlier. What was she doing out there all alone?

I tucked my letter and map in my back pocket and set off into the mess to help that girl. I noticed nearby capsules as best as I could, so that when I found her, I'd know where to go next.

A wall of earth shot up into the sky like a rocket, throwing me on my butt. Huge boulders of rock and dirt cascaded right next to me. I clenched my teeth, got up, and stumbled away.

The earth quaked beneath my feet. The ground jutted upward and propelled me a few yards. I patted down my body and stood back up. It hurt, but my body was still functional.

Above me was the familiar *chop-chop-chopping* of the helicopter. It was really high, though, probably to be out of range of the earth shooting up and smashing into it. A long rope with a hook on the end flung down near me, but I couldn't take it without helping the girl first.

Through the rumbling earth and helicopter blades, I heard the girl calling for help. She was trapped under some fallen rubble. Helping her would put me in extreme danger, but what could I do? Her dark eyes fixed on mine, like I was her last hope.

I ran to the girl, squatted down, and pulled at the stone with all my might. Unfortunately for us both, puberty had yet to bother me much, and I was a bit small for my age. The rock didn't budge. I pulled back and looked at her.

Those dark eyes were accented by the delicate pink of her cheeks and blond hair. But they also had fire in them. Before she looked like a puppy in a store, waiting to be freed; now she looked like she was going to pull up the rubble herself and beat me to death with it in frustration.

I cracked my fingers and tensed for another pull. I dug my hands under the stone and lifted. If I was going to die, at least I'd go out trying to help a beautiful girl. To my surprise the rubble shifted! Then, to my panic, it shot up. The ground beneath had lifted it clear into the stratosphere. The girl fell from the earth, but only a few feet. I took her by the hand, and we stumbled forward and took hold of the helicopter's line.

I anchored my foot in the hook and held on for dear life. The girl positioned her foot on top of mine and held me tightly. Her touch was warm and she smelled sweet like apples.

The girl pulled her hair back and looked at me with those dark eyes. It was too loud to talk, but her smile said it all. If I survived this Upheaval, I couldn't wait to tell my friends back home that not only did I not die on my first day, but that I saved the life of a beautiful girl...even if it was a bit of an embellishment.

We were lowered only a few yards away from the Administration building and the helicopter vanished into the distance. When the earth stopped shaking an all-clear was called over the speakers. I introduced myself to blondie, but before she could thank me for my heroics, Dr. Renner interrupted.

"Tesla, what were you doing out there? I had to stop everything I was doing just because you—"

The girl rolled her eyes and stormed off.

Dr. Renner sighed and turned to me. He was middle-aged, with brown and grey hair. His eyes were dark brown and tired.

"Welcome to the Junkyard," he said, looking me over. "Aren't you a bit small for this kind of work?"

Wow, did he actually see me fail at lifting that stone or what? "My name is Gage Ward, sir. I'm here to be the best Delver you've ever had, small or not."

Dr. Renner's eyes widened. He probably wasn't expecting me to greet him so nicely after his rude remark.

"Very well. I'm Dr. Renner. I was told you had an envelope for me."

I reached behind to retrieve the envelope. Heat erupted in my face as my fingers could grasp nothing but air. I patted down my body in hopes of finding the envelope, but turned up nothing.

And that's where it all started to go wrong. To play any game well, you have to keep your cool, otherwise mistakes get made. It turned out that I had already made a mistake on my first day—in saving the girl, I also lost the envelope, perhaps now hundreds of feet down in the earth.

To make matters worse, it turned out that Dr. Renner was already going to punish me for that mistake.

CHAPTER 3

RELIC HUNT

Delver's Survival Guide Rule #1: Never travel in an Upheaval Zone alone. Risks include but are not limited to: collapsing through the earth, falling rocks, getting stuck in a pit or under a rock, and becoming lost. A partner grants greater safety in such situations.

There was little time to acclimate myself to the new surroundings. There was a quick meal—meatloaf. It tasted like dog-food, but it was still better than the packed lunches my mom would always send me to school with. Tuesday Tofu Tacos got really old, really fast, and no one *ever* traded with me. I didn't blame them; I usually threw most of it away myself. So, even though the meatloaf was dry, burnt, and may not have even contained any real meat, I actually kind of enjoyed it.

The "rolls" that came with it though? Hard as jaw-breakers. Honestly, I don't think scientists could tell the difference between them and regular old rocks.

Lunch was rushed though. It's after an Upheaval that new discoveries about the past civilization can be made, and as a new recruit, this would be my first time excavating. The officials split us all into two groups—the Red Team and the

Blue Team. The rules were simple. The team to find the greatest technology, as determined by Dr. Renner, won.

I couldn't believe my luck; I was on the Red Team with the brown-eyed beauty, Tes. Turned out she was a third-year, a couple years older than me. Best not to get distracted though. I embarrassed myself losing the envelope because I was so busy saving Tes' life, but I couldn't let her soft scent distract me from the greater goal.

There were two others on the team as well. Parker was new like me, and I didn't like that one bit. We needed more experienced members. He was taller than I was and was always moving his hands. He'd slide them through his hair, play with the buttons on his explorer's vest, and hide them in his pockets, but it seemed like they never stayed put for long.

The other was named Wesley, but that's all I knew about him because he was nowhere to be found. The good news was, unlike Parker and me, he'd been here for a couple years. The bad news was that the Blue Team was all senior members of the squad—with no new recruits. More experience equals better results. I knew I'd have to make up for the handicap. They must've put me on this team because of my initial failure to deliver the package. It's hard to blame them. How could I be trusted to secure a Relic if I can't even secure an envelope?

"Alright," Tes said, "going up against Jordan and Nash won't be easy. They're sure to stake their claim to the north, where the last Relic was found."

"Can't we get there first?" Parker asked.

Tes shook her head. "Not without Wesley," Tes said.

"Where is he?" I asked.

"He's on his way," Tes said. "Nash locked him in the broken capsule, again."

"What do you mean?" Parker asked.

Tes pointed behind her. There were a few capsules lined up in the safe-zone. "The capsules are always open and have a sensor on the inside that closes the door. Once inside, you can open the door by placing your hand on a reader. Except that the reader in the broken one doesn't work."

"You mean he's just stuck in there?" Parker asked.

Tes nodded.

"Well, let's get him out," I said.

Tes crossed her arms. "We can't. You need special access to open it up from the outside."

"So Nash did that so we'd be behind on time?" I asked.

"And so they'd get the better excavation site," Tes said.

"That's not fair," I said. "How do we compete if they get the best site?"

"We'll just have to work harder," Tes said.

A boy strolled over to the group from the capsules. His face was red and sweaty. He had the normal explorer's vest on, but he also wore a tattered black hoodie over it. He breathed heavy like he'd been running a marathon, but he just walked the whole way.

"Hey, are you Wesley?" I asked.

The boy stared at me like I'd asked him to eat a bowl of worms.

"No, that's Fido," Parker said. "I heard some other guys talking about him earlier."

The boy turned his glare to Parker. The way he gripped his fists, you'd have thought Parker *called* him a bowl of worms.

"Don't call him Fido," Tes said. "His name is Wesley."

"Then why'd those guys call him Fido?" Parker asked.

Wesley was pretty upset and the sweat seemed to percolate on his forehead all the more.

"Never mind that. They're just jerks," Tes said.

"Nash's worse than a jerk," Wesley said. "And one of these days he's gonna choke on that stupid dog whistle." He wiped his head with the back of his arm and pulled at his ears.

I couldn't help but feel bad for the kid. I hated getting bullied at school, and it sounded like Wesley was getting the brunt of it here. To avoid bullies, I found it best not to stick out too much, and with that hoodie, Wesley looked a bit strange.

"Why don't you take off that hoodie?" I asked. "Maybe you could cool off a little."

Wesley just grunted at me. "Leave me alone. Do I tell you how to dress?"

Tes interrupted. "Knock off the stupid stuff. We've got to figure out how we're going to beat the Blue Team."

Wesley shook his head and sighed. "It's hopeless. They've already got the area to the north. The southern area's been picked completely dry. We may as well find some capsules and get a nap in. This place'll be closing down soon anyway."

I would've punched Wesley in the face if he wasn't the size of a hippo, and apparently just as lazy.

"They may have the first choice, but it's a small area," Tes said. "There's more for us to explore than just the southern section. A larger area might actually work better for us."

That sounded encouraging.

"Do you think we should split up?" Parker asked. "Tes and I can scout the border to the north. There might be good stuff in the vicinity of the Blue Team's area."

Splitting up wasn't a bad idea, but Parker just made my list. No way did I want to team up with Wesley, and I wasn't about to let him hang out with Tes that easy.

"I agree," I said. "But I think Tes should take me back to the area we were exploring earlier today."

Tes held her arm and looked away. "I'm not sure that's a gre—"

"Not so fast," Parker said. "It was my idea, wasn't it? Why shouldn't I get to pick first?"

"Because you're not smart enough," I said.

Wesley groaned. "Typical first-years."

Parker scratched his head. "What do you mean I'm not smart enough? What makes you think that?"

"You can't even keep your hands still. I'll bet your brain is the same way."

"Oh and you're some genius?" Parker asked.

Wesley smirked. Apparently this was all very amusing to him. But not to me. I *was* a genius.

Tes rolled her eyes. "If you two are going to act like this, I'll just go with Wesley."

Wesley shook his head and sat on the ground. "No, no. I want to see how they settle this one. Anyone got some popcorn?"

"Well?" Parker asked.

I pulled the Rubik's cube out of my jacket and held it out to Parker. "Can you solve this?"

"Can you?" Parker countered.

"No problem," I said, and turned it a couple times.

"Not so fast," Parker said. He slid over to me and lifted my hand with the cube into the air and turned it from side to side. He stood so close I could smell his meatloaf-breath.

"What are you doing?" I asked.

"A couple things, one of which is checking this cube," Parker said and moved away. "It looks just fine. Go ahead."

I whizzed the cube in my hands and it was done.

"Wow," Wesley said, clapping. "That'll come in real handy when the Upheavals come."

"Don't worry about Gage during an Upheaval. He's already proved to be both brave and resourceful," Tes said.

"Big deal. Give me the cube," Parker said. "Anyone can do that."

I moved the cube a few times and left just a few squares out of place. "Here's an easy one, then. Let's see if you can do even the easiest of puzzles."

Tes tapped her foot and looked at her watch.

Parker took the cube from me and observed each side. "No problem. And don't worry, Tes, This won't take long. I can do it in six easy moves."

I snickered. The puzzle may have been an easy set-up, but it wasn't even possible in that few moves. "If you pull that off, you win. Good luck doing the impossible."

"Sometimes you just gotta think outside the box," Parker said. He scratched at the cube until one of the colored stickers peeled off. He proceeded to do that with the other out-of-place squares and replaced them to solve the puzzle.

I shook my head. "No. That's cheating."

Parker tossed the cube back. "You never said I couldn't do that. The puzzle's solved, so I win."

"Fine, whatever," Tes said. "Parker and I will take the area southeast of the Blue Team's area. You two will take the southwestern side.

Wesley pushed himself up and dusted off his hands. "I think I'll sit this one out. I'm sure the *genius* can do the job better without me anyway. Do none of you think it'd be better to just take a nap?"

Fire burned up inside me. Sure, I wasn't super excited to be working with the guy, he had an attitude as prickly as a pine cone, but the worst part was that it was going to make us lose. He wasn't even going to lend a hand?

I opened my mouth to give him a piece of my mind when Parker threw up his hands. "No way! We're outgunned by the Blue Team. We need every man we can get."

"Plus, it goes against the rules," I said. "We're not supposed to delve in the Upheaval areas alone."

Wesley pulled his hoodie over his head. "Why're you in such a hurry to risk your lives for Dr. Renner, anyway?"

"If you don't want to help, what're you even doing here?" Parker asked.

In that moment, as much as I hated Parker, I found that I liked him more and more.

Wesley gnashed his teeth and his face reddened. "You have no idea what you're even doing, so don't bother questioning me. If you two want to be pawns for the government, fine. I couldn't care less. But they're gonna ruin the world, and I don't want to be a part of it."

A pawn for the government? I gripped my fingers into fists. As far as I was concerned they were the ones who gave me a chance to get away from home. *I* was using *them* to get what I wanted.

Tes must have seen how upset I was getting, because she put her hand on my shoulder. "Guys, all the bickering is a waste of sunlight." Her hand breathed warmth to my body and her apple-like scent calmed my mind. "It's time to get to work. Wesley, you've been here for just as long as I have. Use this time to teach Gage. I'll do the same with Parker."

Wesley skulked close to me. "Alright. Lesson one, keep your eyes open and don't trust anyone."

Tes shot a cold look at Wesley. Her hand left my shoulder. If felt like a cord being pulled out of a socket. "Why would you say something like that?" Tes asked.

"No one trusted me, so why should anyone trust you, or anyone else?" Wesley asked.

Tes turned away from us in a huff. She put her arm around Parker. "Let's go."

"One last thing," Parker said. He reached in his pocket and pulled out what looked like a chess piece, a king. "Missing anything Mr. Genius?"

I dug into my pocket. It was empty. That was my chess piece! "You thief!"

He tossed it to me and traipsed off with Tes.

Wesley put his arm around me, too. It was safe to say it didn't feel quite as nice as Tes'. "Don't worry about them. They won't be finding anything interesting. None of the others believe me, but I've found something you just *have* to see!"

CHAPTER 4

INTO THE PIT

Delver's Survival Guide Rule #7: Keep plenty of food and water available at all times. Upheavals don't always last long, but getting trapped by rocks or in a safety capsule is common. Rescue teams can take hours or days before finding lost persons.

Wesley drove a load-bearing peg into the earth. A rope was tied to the end of it, which he tossed over the side of a cliff.

"That's where we're going?" I asked.

Wesley nodded.

"What's down there, anyway?" I asked.

"See for yourself." Wesley pulled his hood off his head. His hair was matted to the front of his forehead with sweat.

"Seriously, why do you wear that thing? It's like eighty degrees out here. You should take it off."

He rubbed the back of his neck. "Who're you trying to be, my mom? What's it matter to you? Can't I just wear what I want?"

His words shocked me a second. Not because he was being rude, but because it sounded exactly like something I would say to *my* mom.

"You know what?" I said. "You're right. My parents are always trying to tell me what to wear. Did you know they have certain colors for certain days of the week?"

Wesley's face contorted like he'd just sniffed the air in a crowded bathroom. "You mean like you have to wear blue on Wednesdays? And people call *me* crazy…"

I adjusted my tan adventurer's jacket. "I can't tell you how good it feels not to be wearing Wednesday Reds right now."

Wesley snorted. "You *are* a rebel, aren't you?"

I guess it didn't seem like a big deal to Wesley, but it was a big deal for me. Everything in my life was scheduled and controlled. Some people have OCDs about washing their hands or making sure everything is in even numbers. My parents' OCD was everything in my life—what I wore, what I ate. Everything.

"It's not about being a rebel, it's just about having a little bit of breathing room," I said.

"And you thought this was the best place to come for that?"

"Of course. I wanted to be here."

"And your parents? They wanted you here, too?"

It was probably the last thing they wanted. My dad thought being a dentist would be the best thing for me. I think my mom just wanted me to be happy—which sounds nice, except that she thinks what makes her happy is what should make me happy.

"Let's just say my parents don't really know what's going on," I said.

24

Wesley chuckled. "You parents don't know that you've joined one of the most dangerous groups in the world for kids our age?"

"They think I'm going to some summer camp," I said.

"There's no way your parents are so stupid. And there's no way the government would allow you to put your life on the line without your parents signing off on it."

My fingers singed with heat. Wesley obviously didn't believe me and it bothered me. That's why I let my secret slip. "My parents did sign off on it...kind of. I mean, I forged their signatures."

A huge grin stretched on Wesley's face. "All that just to come here? To the Junkyard?"

"At least here I can do what I want," I said.

"All you'll find here are more people using you to get what they want," Wesley said, motioning to the pit.

The cavern extended down into blackness. "What's down there anyway?" I asked.

"Something bigger and better than the Blue Team will ever find, that's for sure. I've been working on unearthing it for a few days."

"Why didn't you say anything about this before?" I asked.

"It's just like I told you before, I don't trust any of them," Wesley said.

"So why're you suddenly putting your faith in me?" I asked.

"I don't have anyone else to turn to and I can't waste any more time. The Upheaval could've buried all the work I've put in trying to unearth that thing. If I try and do it alone, I may never get it out."

It sounded like winning the competition would be easier than I thought. I grabbed the rope and began my descent. "Okay. Let's go get it," I said.

Wesley grabbed the rope and started climbing down above me. He was a bit slower than I was, though. His breathing was labored. It was kind of weird that someone who'd been doing this for years was in as bad of shape as he was.

"Sorry, I've never been very good at this part," Wesley said.

"No problem," I said. "See ya at the bottom."

When I reached the floor of the pit I realized two things: one, I couldn't hear Wesley's breathing anymore, and two, I would not, in fact, be seeing Wesley at the bottom, or anything else.

He'd tricked me.

CHAPTER 5

DISCOVERY

Delver's Survival Guide Rule #3: Rope is necessary for safely delving into pits. Load-bearing pegs must be connected for safe descents.

By the time I'd climbed all the way back up the ropes, my arms burned from the exercise. But it was nothing compared to how hot my temper was.

Wesley was nowhere in sight and he'd wasted almost half-an-hour of my time. Worst of all, he'd left me completely abandoned in the Upheaval zone. It's not like I'm a huge fan of rules or anything, but when breaking them puts my life in danger, it kind of makes me want to leave *him* at the bottom of a random pit.

I took in a deep breath of cold air and closed my eyes. I imagined the air moving through me and tickling my fingers and toes with its chill. I had to calm down. Getting angry leads to making mistakes.

I opened my eyes and blew out my negative thoughts.

Okay, where did he go?

Did he go back to Tes and Parker? Did he actually go back to the safe-zone to get a nap?

I took my knife and dug out the peg I'd used to climb down into the pit.

I grabbed a baseball-sized piece of earth that came out with the peg. Its round shaped reminded me of Wesley's stupid fat stomach.

If I was a lying, lazy, hoodie-wearing lunatic who didn't trust anyone, where would I go?

I tossed the ball of earth off the cliff. Part way on its journey down it cracked into the side of the cliff and something came into my mind.

There was something odd about what Wesley had said earlier. He mentioned that the southern area had been excavated in full and was completely cleaned out of Relics.

Just as the rock hit the bottom of the pit the truth hit me—Wesley *did* find something!

He wasn't napping in his capsule and he wasn't helping me because he must've found something in the southern site that he didn't want to share. I would've bet my nose hairs that Wesley was down south, trying to unearth something awesome. And he'd even fooled me—at least, for a little while. Luckily, I still had plenty of time to catch him, and when I did, I'd also find a Relic that would put the Red Team on the map. Sure, Wesley wouldn't be happy about it, but it was his fault for being selfish anyway.

I dashed south. The campgrounds were an odd assortment of manmade architecture and towers of rock from earlier Upheavals. The massive pillars made me feel quite insignificant and very mortal. I guess that's why only certain people sign up for gigs like this, but it was certainly worth it for me. Anything to get away from home.

Amongst the rocks and cliffs was a cave, burrowing deep into the earth. It wasn't like any other cavern. It seemed fairly unaffected by the Upheaval. Could this be the place?

I pulled out my flashlight and climbed down. The air was metallic and cold in my nostrils. Peaking between the rocks was metal on the ground. There was no sight of Wesley yet, but it was a deep cave, stretching down far into the earth. Someone had spent a lot of time carving out this path.

After some time, it was so quiet I could've heard a butterfly fart. Unfortunately, that probably meant I was in the wrong place—Wesley wasn't here. If he was, I would've heard his heavy panting by now. Still, this was the most interesting place I'd seen so far.

My plan to find Wesley was put on hold when I saw something glimmer on the ground. At first it just looked like a metal pen, but when I knelt down I saw that it had two faders on the side of it. I grabbed and inspected it. I pushed one fader up, but it didn't seem to do anything. If it was a Relic, maybe it needed some kind of ancient battery or something. But I was wrong.

When I pushed the second fader, a beam of light shot out of it. I waved the metal-thingy around and watched the dot of light dance on the walls. Neat, I guess. At least it didn't need ancient batteries. But honestly, I wasn't impressed. You could buy laser pointers at Walmart for a buck or two. It did have one advantage over those designs though—its beam of light could sustain itself in any color, where modern pointers are always red.

I could see it now. My career would skyrocket as the US government taps all the potential found in a multi-color laser pointer. At least boring board meetings would have point-five-percent more pizazz.

No, this wasn't a great find, but I pocketed the pointer. At least if the Blue Team found nothing, we'd win by comparison. It's kind of like the food here. Sure, meatloaf is awful, but it's still better than Tofu Taco Tuesday.

The cavern didn't so much end as narrow to the point I could no longer progress. Large rocks were stacked against each other. I could tell there was more behind them, but I couldn't make any progress. I fell to my hands and knees and peeked my flashlight though a small hole at the bottom, but it was just too narrow for me to see beyond.

My guess, this was Wesley's cave and he was hiding something.

And I was going to find out what it was.

CHAPTER 6

REFLECTIONS

Delver's Survival Guide Rule #4: Relics must be treated with upmost care. Technologies discovered must be declared safe by the USDS before use.

Tes and Parker bounded over a hill. "You're not going to believe it," Tes said.

It sounded like good news. Had she and Parker found something great? I played around with the light-pen in my pocket, wondering whether to say anything, but I decided against it.

When they reached me, Parker peered past me with a puzzled look on his face. Tes just shook her head.

"Where's Wesley?" Parker asked.

Where Wesley went *was* important, but not as important as the news they seemed to have.

"I dunno," I said. "He ditched me. But what happened with you guys? What won't I believe?"

"The Blue Team found something amazing," Tes said.

What? It felt like my stomach dug a hole to China. Why was this good news? "So, we lost?" I asked.

Tes nodded.

"Unless you and Wesley found something," Parker said.

I had, but it didn't sound like it measured up to *something amazing*. "We didn't find a single thing," I said. "But I think Wesley's hiding something...big."

Tes crossed her arms. "Sometimes I think so too, but I've never found anything."

"I might have. Inside a cave, but there was a barrier I couldn't get past," I said.

Tes crinkled her nose, which was as cute as a bunny. "Really?" she asked.

"Well it doesn't matter now," Parker said. "Time's been called. Even if we found something, it'd be too late for the competition."

"So what'd they find that was so amazing anyway?" I asked. "And why'd it make you so happy if it means we lost?"

Tes smiled at me, those brown eyes shining. Uncomfortable sweat percolated under my arms. She's too much. I gotta focus.

"It'll make my dad happy," Tes said.

Sure it would make Dr. Renner happy, but certainly not me. I guess between Tes being happy about losing and Wesley not giving a crap, only Parker and I would be disappointed at all.

Parker put his arm behind me and we slumped towards the bad news together.

Over the hill I heard the Blue Team cheer and slap hands in celebration.

While I was bummed about losing, I did feel the electric in my body to see what could be worth celebrating so greatly.

Tes raced up the hill, and against my poor spirits I found myself joining her. Besides the laser-pointer in my pocket, this would be the first Relic I'd ever seen.

We arrived to see a whole slew of gorillas dressed in blue, at least that's how big they were and how they acted. They beat their chests and high-fived, shouting things like, "Aww-yeah!" and "Whoo-hoo!" like a bunch of crazies.

If I'd ground my teeth any harder, they'd probably shatter. I was jealous, sure, but I was more angry than jealous. How was it fair to put all these guys (and I think one of them was a girl) into one group together, give them the best site, and put them up against a team of newbies?

But it wasn't them I was interested in anyway; it was the Relic. Honestly, I was underwhelmed. It was just a panel on the ground. It had a foot-switch and two little holes in it.

"Hey, Tes!" one gorilla said. "C'mon over here! You're gonna love this."

Did I say I was more mad than jealous? Well that was premature, because when Tes traipsed over and the gorilla put his arm around her, I felt like my stomach was being mixed in a blender.

Then she kissed his cheek!

Parker's jaw dropped, probably for the same reason as mine did—and I'm pretty sure it wasn't because of the "awesome" Relic, either.

"So Nash," Tes said, each word kicking my stomach in. "What'd you guys find?"

Nash squinted, surveyed our team, and chuckled. "Hey, where's Fido?"

Tes shoved him. "You gotta stop putting him in that chamber. My dad's looking for a reason to kick you out of here."

"Maybe," Nash said. "But not after he sees what I unearthed."

"Well, what is it?" she asked.

"Oh it's great. You gotta see this," he said, walking up to the foot-switch. She staggered behind, being pulled along by her hand. "Don't be scared, we've all tried it and nothing bad happens."

Nash pressed down the switch. From the two holes in front of him, beams of electric light shot out with a static-like *Verwhoosh*. The beams of light rounded out and met about seven feet in the air in the shape of an oval.

I dug in my pocket. Yup, it was way cooler than the light-pen.

The light streams from the beams funneled into the middle of the oval, and that's when we saw the most intriguing part. Standing beyond Nash in the electric oval was a lion!

I jolted like I'd been doused with freezing water.

"Nash, look out!" Tes said, stumbling back.

He just laughed. His voice was deep, confident, and annoying. "Don't worry, babe, it doesn't move unless I do. It's like a mirror."

He was right. He stepped back and so did the lion.

"You know what's the weird part?" Nash asked, grinning as wide as a banana. "It'll be different for you." He took Tes by the hand and led her to the mirror. Looking back at her was not a girl anymore, but a wolf. She staggered back from the mirror with her hand over her mouth.

"Don't run away," Nash said, grabbing at her hands.

"Stop it," Tes said, swatting him away.

"C'mon, I want to see you in the mirror a little closer. It's not dangerous."

I shot out, "Stop it, jerk." Nash's eyes darted at me. He let Tes' hand slip from his grasp and angled his massive body towards me.

I swallowed nervous saliva mixed with immediate regret. He *was* a lion, and now I was his prey.

"What'd you say, boy?" Nash asked.

My head sunk into my shoulders and I wished I were a turtle. At least then it could sink all the way out of view. Tes looked concerned, but she had a glimmer of a smile on her face. Sticking up for her felt good, but the consequences sure wouldn't.

Nash loomed over me. "Speak up, kid. Didn't you hear me?"

I nodded. Saving Tes from the Upheaval seemed far less scary than Nash's fists banging my face.

He grabbed my shoulders.

Tes yelled, "Leave him alone, Nash."

"Calm down, will ya?" He moved me like a chess piece in front of the mirror. "I just want to see what the mirror has to say about our new friend here."

Everyone snickered. Everyone except Tes and Parker, that is. Nash just shook his head. Then I understood why. In front of the lion that was Nash, stood a tiny mouse, not even tall enough to stand over Nash's paw.

"You'd think he would've been a bull or something, the way he butted in," Nash said. "But a little mouse? Well, Mickey Mouse, for a little guy you sure have a big mouth."

More laughs from the idiots in the crowd. It felt like it was coming from everywhere. It usually wouldn't have bothered me. I'd been picked on plenty in school. But being laughed at in front of a girl, especially a girl like Tes, made me do something—something very stupid.

"Shut up, meathead," I said and shoved Nash. He stumbled back half a step, his eyes wide probably more from shock than actual fear.

He smiled and shook his head. "Dumb move, Mickey Mouse." He punched me in the gut. It hit so hard I think I lifted clear off the ground before crashing into it.

"Nash! Stop it!" Tes shouted. "Gage's my friend."

I know it shouldn't have, but the word *friend* was a like a second harsh punch to the gut. Still, her sympathy was welcomed. I hopped to my feet and jumped on his back. I tried squeezing his pressure points, but his shoulders were harder than the rolls served with lunch. He just laughed, which irritated me even more. It's one thing to be weak, it another to have your weakness paraded in front of everyone.

Nash elbowed me in the sides and I fell off.

"You'll stay on the ground this time," he said. He turned and dashed at me.

I swiveled around and darted off, but Nash's head start gave him the upper hand. His hand pounded on my shoulder.

The electric mirror was getting closer. In it, I could see the mouse racing towards me, being chased down by the lion.

I was on a collision course, so I buckled. But Nash gave me one big push.

I rolled on the ground and felt the light from the mirror flood over me. It kind of felt like taking a hot shower, only from the inside out. When I looked up, it appeared I'd missed the mirror after all—I sat right in front of it.

But I knew better. I went right through the thing.

The weird part was that everything looked bigger. My body felt light and the cool wind snapped at me like I wasn't wearing any clothes.

Everyone stared at me, and it didn't take me long to realize that it wasn't because I'd just made a stupid fool of myself—it was because I came out the other side of the mirror in the form of a mouse!

CHAPTER 7

BAD NEWS

Delver's Survival Guide Rule #6: Capsules are fortified to undergo extreme pressure, but retain their shape. Their design makes them durable and transportable. Capsules are the safest place to be in the event of an Upheaval.

The good news was that going through the mirror was a two-way process. The bad news was the fact that I'd completely embarrassed myself in front of Tes, picked a fight with the biggest brute here, and on top of that, failed to win the competition.

I plopped myself on my bed and pressed the "containment" button. The lid of the small chamber closed over me. It was designed for safety during an Upheaval, but it felt like a coffin, which given my track record for today, seemed appropriate. I dug in my pocket and pulled out my light-pen. I turned it on and drew squiggles on the top of the sleeping chamber. I pressed up and down on the other fader, but like last time, it didn't seem to do anything.

I turned off the pen and closed my eyes. Today sucked, but at least tomorrow held new opportunities. I'd been in losing chess positions before, but the key was to claw your way back.

It would take careful tactics and more focus, but I knew where I'd failed today. I'd let Tes' smile distract me. I'd leave her to Nash. Maybe he'd lose his focus too.

I smiled and took in a deep breath.

Just as I neared sleep, a light turned on and the lid of my sleeping chamber slipped open over me. I sat up to see if it was malfunctioning, but it was Parker and Tes.

Parker's eyes were wide and darted around and he was ringing his hands like he was constantly washing them. Tes was in these fluffy pink pajamas. They weren't very cute, or soft looking. And she definitely didn't smell like apples.

"Gage, there's some really bad news," Parker said.

Okay, she did smell like warm apples, but I was definitely refocused. Her pink cheeks and dark eyes couldn't distract me anymore.

"Uh, hello?" Parker asked, waving his hand in front of me.

I grabbed his arm. "What'd you say?"

"Gage, there's some big news," Tes said.

"Bad news," Parker added.

I let go of Parker's arm and lay back down. "Can it wait 'til morning? I was just getting to sleep."

Parker shook his head. "No, you don't understand. They're sending us home."

I shot up so fast I almost toppled out of my capsule. "Wait, what?"

Tes nodded. "It's true. They're calling in the big guns now. That Relic Nash found must've really wowed them." Tes' eyes veered off as she mentioned Nash's name. Parker must've seen it too because he was just shaking his head.

"What do you mean?" I asked. "I thought we *were* the big guns?"

Both Tes and Parker looked at me like I'd asked them why the sky was blue.

"Why are you guys looking at me like that?" I asked. "I know Parker and I are just first years, but why kick us all out?"

Parker looked at Tes. "He doesn't know, does he?"

"Know what?"

Tes' eyes widened like she'd just remembered she left the stove on. She nodded her head. "Oh yeah…he didn't get a proper tour. Nobody's told him…"

Parker snapped his fingers. "That's right."

"Out with it already," I said. "Nobody told me what?"

"This place is the dumping ground for Delvers," Tes said. "That's why it's called 'The Junkyard.' We're basically benchwarmers waiting for a chance to prove ourselves in the hope of getting stationed at a real excavation site."

I shook my head. I couldn't believe it. Why would they put me in the worst site? Mr. Brown-suit must've made a mistake. And now I was losing my chance already. They'd be sending me home after one measly day? "So we're getting sent home now?" I asked.

"That's their plan," Parker said, shoving his hands in his pockets.

"But we have a better one," Tes said, smiling.

Anything would be better than getting sent home. "What do you have in mind?"

Tes moved close. Her warm scent filled the air around me. She whispered, "You said you thought Wesley found something, right? Something big?"

Her eyes and smile were fiendish and I kind of liked it. "Yeah, but I ran into a dead end. I don't know how to get past it," I said.

Parker joined the huddle. "Don't you have any idea?"

I shook my head. "Maybe we should interrogate Wesley for some info."

Tes and Parker shook their heads in unison. "We thought to do that ourselves a few minutes ago," Tes said, "but when we got to his dorm he was having one of his episodes."

"One of his what?" I asked.

"He gets this way sometimes," Tes said. "He was yelling and screaming. We thought if he knew that we were being kicked out, he'd want to help us, but he wouldn't open his door at all."

That struck me as odd. Wesley didn't seem to be the flip-a-switch yelling and screaming kind of guy, especially with no provocation. But then again, I'd only met him once.

"That's when we came here to talk to you," Parker said.

"And you're all we have to go on now, Gage," Tes said "So…do you have any ideas?"

I'm not going to lie. The confidence Tes put in me mixed with the hope in her eyes made me really want to find a solution. It was a tough puzzle alright, but like Mr. Brown-suit's Rubik's Cube challenge, I was ready to exceed expectations under time-pressure.

And that's when I had a great and horrible idea, but one that just might work. "I'll need both of your help for this one. I hope you're good actors."

CHAPTER 8

DISTRACTION

Delver's Survival Guide Rule #9: Cell wave interference in and around the Upheaval Zone render Cell phones useless. Their use has been prohibited by the USDS. There is no 911 and you cannot call home. Your team is your security.

I crouched in the shadows. Around the slab of earth that hid me was the Blue Team's Relic. Two of the Junkyard's officers stood guard in front of it. Not because anyone wanted to steal it—it would be excessively cumbersome to move. No, they just didn't want it being damaged, which became a real concern the moment I whizzed right through it.

Tes' voice echoed in the distance. "Let it go! It's mine!"

"I just want to look at it. Take it easy, will ya?" Parker answered.

They passed in front of me and continued walking nearby the Relic. Tes grabbed Parker and threw him to the ground. "You're a rotten thief. My dad'll have you expelled for this," she said.

"We're all getting booted out anyway, so what's it matter, you blond-haired Barbie."

Tes' eyes widened and she pulled Parker close by his jacket. "Oh, now you've done it. When I tell my dad, he'll—"

"Hey! Break it up!" an officer said, pulling them apart. "What's the problem?"

The officers separated Parker and Tes and one stood in front of each.

Tes pointed past the guard. "He stole a Relic from my dad!"

Parker shook his head. "No, you said it was yours!"

"Where d'ya think I got it, slug brain?" Tes asked.

The guards shot worried glances at each other and nodded.

"Where is it now," the guard in front of Parker asked.

"Yeah Parker. Where'd ya hide it?" Tes echoed.

Parker flashed a grin. "You'll never guess. I've got it somewhere no one'll ever find."

"Oh, right next to your brain then?" Tes asked.

Parker lunged at her, but the guard pushed him back.

"Funny! You think I'm stupid, at least I'm not dating the dumbest meat-head here." Parker's face was red, and so was Tes'. If this was all an act, they were certainly selling it.

The guard shook Parker. "Where's the Relic, pipsqueak?"

Parker harrumphed.

"If you don't get it from him, I'll tell my dad," Tes said.

The guards shared the same worried glance again.

"Last chance, kid."

Parker smiled. "I hid it in Wesley's capsule. Good luck finding it in all the clutter."

The guard dropped Parker, who crashed to the ground. "Go get it," the guard said.

"You can't trust him," Tes said. "You gotta go with him."

"No. We're here to watch the Relic, not babysit a couple kindergartners."

Tes stomped her foot and stormed off. "I'm telling my dad. You'll be sorry."

Parker ran off too. "See ya! Now that Barbie's gone I can go get the Relic back."

The guards looked at each other one last time and sighed. They clenched their fists, and darted off, one after Tes, the other after Parker.

Now was my chance. I stepped on the trigger and activated the mirror with a loud *Verwhoosh*! Sure the officers may have heard it, but it wouldn't matter. Even if they did, by the time they got back, they'd never find a little mouse in all the rocks.

Chapter 9

The World Before

Step one of my plan went perfectly, but step two was another story. I hadn't factored in the fact that I'd have to travel the same distance to the cave, but in a smaller body. In chess it only takes a rook one move to go all the way across the board, but it takes a pawn at least five. The good news is when the pawn *does* get to the other side, it gets to turn into a different piece. The bad news was that it might not be true for me.

The world is different as a mouse. It's like when you grow up and see your baby toys again. They all seemed so much bigger when you were small. Having my face at ground-level allowed me to see much of the ignored world. I never realized that bugs are everywhere! And I kind of wished I hadn't found that out either.

It was later than I'd expected, but I arrived back at the cave. The metallic smell was even greater, especially since I realized the floor itself was earth mixed with metal. When I'd been wearing shoes I didn't realize how cold parts of the ground were, but now that I was walking with tiny bare feet, I could tell the metallic foundation apart from the rocks.

At the end of the cave was the rocky barrier, but now that I was barely larger than a golf ball, the restraints didn't limit me nearly as much. My tiny heart beat quickly inside with the thoughts of finding a Relic that might give us a chance to prove ourselves.

I squeezed through the narrow space between the boulders and the floor and a low humming pervaded the air. I actually felt it more than heard it. It was like my tiny organs were all vibrating inside of me.

The end of the tunnel was darkness and while my heart was still pounding, it was now out of fear that I'd reached the end, and would have nothing to show for it.

I'd never been so wrong in my life.

The room was massive, and not just because I was still a mouse. It was completely dark still, but the outlines were definitely mechanical. Metallic panels on the ceiling and walls had the shape of hexagons, kind of like a bee's honeycomb. The humming was pervasive and shook my bones. It would've been alarming if it didn't cause a warming, calming sensation inside my stomach.

While dark, there were dim lights emitting from the panels on the ceiling and walls. It was like the walls themselves were giving off the vibrations as well as the light.

I skittered towards the center of the room where there was a glasslike tile. Coming near to it, I discovered the intricacies in the glass. Each frame was the size of sand, but had crystalline patterns. I pushed against it, but there wasn't the smallest movement. In this form I had no strength.

I moved on to a lightly illuminated wall. On the way the ground shifted beneath me and a familiar *Verwhoosh* sounded, complete with light beams forming a large mirror, with myself standing on the other side. Another mirror.

I happily jumped through and was my normal self again.

I pressed down the switch, powering down the mirror and went to the wall. A small table held a number of strange trinkets. They looked like metal pins like you'd find on a syringe. There was also a metal glove. It wasn't as heavy as I'd thought it would be. It was cold though, especially when I put it on. It made my fingers feel like steel. If it did anything special besides that, I couldn't figure it out.

Following along the wall, I found nothing of interest, so I sat down to think.

I pulled the light-pen out of my pocket and idly turned on the light. That's when things got weird.

Depending on the color of the light, it seemed to connect with something like a hexagonal web of light in the middle of the air. As I moved the fader up or down, the color would change and the light would scatter in the web closer or farther away from me. I had no idea what it meant, but there was some kind of invisible matrix of information in the air.

Just out of curiosity I tried the other fader as well.

But again, there didn't seem to be any response, at least not immediately.

I stood up and turned off the pen.

Just then the low humming of the metal rose in register to a high-pitched buzz, then transposed beyond my ability to hear. The walls illuminated themselves at the same time making the dome so dazzlingly bright that it blinded me. I staggered back, trying to shield my eyes.

"You look lost," a voice said. It was feminine and young, but when I looked I couldn't see anything but white.

"Who are you?" I asked.

The light faded a bit.

Standing in front of me was a girl. Her skin was radiant. Literally, just like the light reflecting from the intricate glass in the middle of the room. She was clothed in white light and her eyes were a warm almond color as was her hair, which snuggled her shoulders.

"Wha...who..." I stammered.

She smiled. "It's okay. I'm Kat."

I couldn't break my gaze from Kat's shimmering smile. She was unlike anyone, or anything, I'd ever seen before. "What are you?"

"I'm what's left of the world before."

"The world before what?"

"The world before your world."

This was amazing. I didn't just find a Relic, I found someone who was actually from the age of all the Relics. The weird thing was that her body's slender frame appeared to be like a sixteen year-old's. "How'd you survive all this time?" I asked.

She motioned me towards the glass pit. "There's a life source down there. It's where I get all of my energy. It's also what's able to generate the light and sound from the Barrix."

"Barrix?" I asked.

"It's the metal this cave is built from," she said.

I moved to the pit in the middle of the room. There was darkness as far down as I could see. What kind of life source would be down there? "How deep does it go?"

"Almost all the way to the center of the earth."

"But that's not even possible," I said.

Kat's eyes sharpened on me. "Five minutes ago you were a mouse scurrying around, and now you're a human being. Would you have ever thought that possible?"

She moved closer to me as she finished her statement, and my underarms clammed up. She was definitely right. At that moment, I was not the authority on what was possible and what wasn't. I stammered, "You're right…sorry. So what exactly's down there anyway?"

A glimmer flashed in her eyes and her lips curled slightly. "There's a creature that hibernates in the middle of the earth. The problem is, it's waking up before its time."

"A creature? Nothing could live down there. The heat would roast it."

Kat shook her head. "You really think you're smart, but I've never heard anyone quite as foolish as you. The creature doesn't live in the heat, it creates the heat. It draws in the nutrients of the earth and dreams the world into being. Everything in this world is born of the dreams of this beautiful creature."

It all sounded crazy, but she was the first girl I'd ever met that seemed to be made of light too, so I wasn't sure what to think. But if it was all true, something bothered me. "If all the life on earth is just a dream, what happens when the creature wakes up?"

"That's what the earthquakes are. When it wakes, it releases its energy in violence, destroying the previous world. Then it will settle itself to sleep again and dream into being the next age."

"How do you know all of this?" I asked.

"Because I watched it happen to my world."

"But if it destroys everything when it wakes up, how did you survive?"

"Both I and this room were built to keep the creature happily asleep forever. The indestructible metals withstand the Upheavals. This pit was my connection to the creature, but I failed to keep it asleep."

"How? What happened?" I asked

"There was a brief overload of the Barrix," she said. "If it expends its energy for light or sound too greatly, it will go dark while it gathers its energy again, much like the creature itself."

This metal sounded amazing. It could illuminate, resonate, *and* it was indestructible? "Where'd you get this metal, anyway?" I asked.

"Like a snake sheds its skin, so does the creature. Its skin is the metal my world used to fashion this room.

"And that's how you survived? Because this place cannot be destroyed by the Upheavals?"

She nodded.

"But wait," I said, "if everything's created in a dream, why didn't it all vanish when it woke up? Why does it matter if you're in a Barrix-laden room when it's all just make-believe anyway?"

"This creature isn't like us. When we dream, it's all just images in our minds, but when it dreams, it radiates energy and life into the earth itself. Its dreamings inhabit the same world it does, and they will continue to do so until their energy is taken from them by time or force. At some point, everything dies."

"Even the creature? Will it die too?"

The girl laughed. "It's far from dying. Compared to you, it's basically eternal."

"But what if we kill it?"

"Why would you want to do that?" she asked. "Even if you could, it's not a good idea. The world would live on for a little while, but with the source of life gone, earth will become like the other planets in the Solar System—dead orbs flying around with no one to enjoy them."

"Then what are we supposed to do?" I asked. "If it's waking up early, it'll destroy my world. Honestly, I've already had kind of a rough day."

"When the people of my age discovered the creature, they created me to do two things: access the power of the creature to help the world, and keep the creature asleep. That's what we can do."

"How does that involve me?" I asked.

"Something was taken from me, by a boy named Wesley."

I knew Wesley'd been hiding something, but I would've never guessed it was something this big. "What'd he take?"

"A circuit from the core in the pit. Without it, my connection with the creature is unstable. Even the power I'm drawing from it now to talk to you is likely to cause an Upheaval."

"So you need me to bring it back to you?"

"I need you to bring *him* back to me."

"Wesley...Why?"

"I like having him around. He reminds me of someone…it gets lonely here to be honest. But mainly, I need him to repair the connection for me. He's a very accomplished engineer. Well beyond his years."

"Say I bring you the circuit. Why can't you fix it yourself?"

She moved close to me and ran her fingers into my body. "I'm just light. I can't touch anything."

I took a step back. "I see. Why'd Wesley leave in the first place? Didn't he know the risk?"

The light from the walls shimmered a second, like a quick shot of lightning. "The prolonged exposure to the pit caused him mental duress. He'd started hearing things. He blamed me for it and tricked me one night. He stole away and blew up the entrance to the cave, afraid I'd come after him."

"Would you have gone after him?"

"It's impossible. I'm confined to this room."

"So I just need to bring him back?"

"That's all. I'll be able to convince him to continue the project. He really is quite a genius, and I know he'll listen to the sound of reason when spoken in the right way."

It all sounded good in theory, but the entrance was sealed off with the rubble. "One more problem," I said. "How'll I be able to get him in through *that*? I was only able to get in earlier because I was a mouse."

"I could turn you back into a mouse, if you like," she said. "But then again, it would be hard to bring Wesley back. I'd suggest just using that," she said, pointing to the glove on my hand.

"Is this made of Barrix, too?" I asked, flexing my fingers. She nodded.

My fingers were chilled and felt mechanical. "What's it do besides making me feel like a cyborg?"

"See for yourself. Go touch the rocks that block the entrance."

I dashed to the entrance and rested my hand on a boulder. Nothing happened.

"I think this one's broken," I said.

"You must first activate it," she said.

I ran my fingers over the surface of the glove. There were no switches or buttons, but there was a slim groove just over the back side of my hand.

"How do I do that?" I asked. "I'm not from your time, so I'm not sure how all this stuff works."

"The key's in your pocket," she said.

I pulled the light-pen out. It was the perfect fit for the groove in the glove. I slid it in and turned on both faders. The glove illuminated a vibrant bluish green, almost like the ocean.

"Now try," she said.

I grabbed the boulders again. This time, they glided like leaves in the wind. My hand repulsed from the rock, not because of the glove, but because it startled me how easily the rocks moved.

Kat smirked like a mom whose child learned a new trick. "That should solve that problem, huh?" she asked.

"How's this thing work?" I asked.

"It reads a substance's mass, then absorbs its atoms briefly, restoring them every millisecond. It repeats this process until the connection is lost."

Chemistry wasn't exactly my favorite subject, but I was pretty sure that that wasn't possible, but then again as Kat kept pointing out, I *was* a mouse today. "So, I didn't really move the rock, it just kept materializing slightly further away every millisecond?"

Kat's eyes widened a bit as she nodded. "Not bad for a child," she said. "In our world, you may have been someone special."

She probably meant it as a compliment, but all I heard was that I wasn't anyone special in this world. I mean, even Wesley was more important than I was. Kat needed him to save the world. I was just the delivery man. "Thanks," I said. "Don't worry, I'll be back with Wesley soon."

The lights began to dim and Kat faded like a ghost. "Remember, he won't want to come. He'll say anything to make you stop. Don't listen to him; your world's fate is at stake."

CHAPTER 10

BETRAYED

My heart beat hard as I dashed out of the cave. The night air was cold in my lungs, but my fingers felt even colder. I removed the glove. What a relief! The whole time it felt like my fingers had turned into metal, but they looked perfectly normal. I blew out a sigh.

The return trip to the safe-zone was much faster in my normal body, but the first person I ran into wasn't anyone I expected to see.

"Hey Mickey, wandering a little far from your clubhouse, aren't you?" Nash asked.

My mouth dropped when I saw him. Not because I was surprised to see Nash—although I was—but because instead of his goons flanking him on either side, there was only Tes.

"What're you doing out so late anyway?" Nash asked.

Tes looked away from me and crossed her arms, and my guess was it wasn't because she was cold.

"What're *you* doing out so late?" I countered, standing tall and tucking the glove into my jeans behind my back. "I thought gorillas slept at night."

Nash closed the gap and towered over me. "Tes and I were having an interesting conversation about the Red Team's plan to win the contest. But as far as I'm concerned the contest's over."

Why would Tes have told him about that? She stood behind Nash and out of my line of vision. "I'm just out for a jog in the fresh air. Y'know, it's been an upsetting day."

Nash grabbed my shirt and pulled me close. I could smell the sweat from his damp clothing. "Jogging in jeans? I don't think so." He reached behind my back, then gave me a quick shove. I tripped to the ground.

"Stop," Tes said. "You said you wouldn't hurt him."

I jumped up and felt the back of my jeans. It was gone.

"I won't," Nash said, holding a glove in front of his face. "So is this what you found, Mickey?"

"Give it back, ya baboon!" I yelled.

Nash slid it on and held it out towards me. "What's it do, anyway?"

I jumped at him and grabbed for it, but missed and fell on my face.

Tes grabbed his shoulder and tried to pull him back. He turned and grabbed her with the glove. Tes screamed.

I bolted to my feet. "Give it back, moron. You don't even know what it does."

Nash kicked me to the ground and inspected the glove, jabbing it with his fingers.

"Leave him alone," Tes said.

"Those aren't buttons, moron," I said. "Give it back."

Nash obviously didn't know how to activate the glove, which was good for Tes, because I have no idea what that thing would do with a human body. It might not kill someone, but having all your mass sucked up and spit back out probably didn't feel pleasant either.

Nash grabbed me. "Thanks for the Relic, Mickey. I'd love to repay you for it, but I can't just let you go free now can I? You sure you don't want to tell me what this thing does?" He flashed a grin at me. "It'd be a shame if you accidently got locked in that broken capsule."

I wasn't born yesterday. He'd be locking me in the capsule whether I told him what the glove did or not. I didn't care at all that I wouldn't get to show off the glove to Tes' dad and win some respect for the Red Team. No, the problem was much bigger. If I got locked up, I wouldn't be able to get Wesley to Kat, and that meant really bad news for everybody. So I said the only thing I could think of to change Nash's mind.

I told him the truth.

"Look Nash. I'm on a very important mission. If I fail, the Upheavals are gonna get really bad and destroy not just a city here and a town there, they're gonna destroy the whole world. You can keep the glove for all I care, just let me go. Please."

The look of surprise on Nash's face was shared by Tes. The only difference was that Nash smiled and laughed. "Can you believe this guy, Tes? He's on a team with Fido for one day and he's already talking crazy like him!"

The look of surprise didn't fade from Tes' face.

Nash carried me off. I kicked and wriggled, but it was useless.

By the time we reached the capsule, I tried one more time to reason with my captors, well one of them anyway. I knew Nash was a lost cause, but maybe Tes could help.

"Tes, you've gotta help me. This is serious!"

She shook her head, but wouldn't look at me.

"Whose side are you on, anyway?" I asked.

Tes' face went red and she scratched her nose. She whispered, "I'm with him."

Nash threw me into the chamber and the last thing I saw was Tes mouth the words, "I'll come for you."

At least, that's what I think she was trying to say. Why would she lie about being on Nash's side? Or was it even a lie?

The door shut with a loud clank.

My fate was sealed, and unfortunately for everyone else, so was theirs.

My heart pounded hard and against all logic a thought popped into my head and made me want to vomit—if the world's going to end, at least the last thing I saw was Tes.

Chapter 11

Trapped

The capsule was dark and smelled like mold. In addition to not being fixed, it probably didn't get cleaned very often either. The lights didn't work, so I pulled out my flashlight.

Or what was left of it.

Nash's less-than-gentle treatment of me when he tossed me in the capsule cracked the darn thing pretty badly. I flipped the switch, but no luck and no light.

I dug in my pocket. At least I still had some form of light. I took out the light-pen and shot its tiny beam on the walls, but it was about as useful for seeing my surroundings as a straw was for giving an elephant a drink. The only good thing it could do was show how close things were. It saved me from bumping my head at least once, so I had to count that as a win.

I pocketed the pen, sat on the floor, and stared at nothingness. Even *if* there was a way out of here, it would be impossible without light. Why the hell did they even keep this place? They could at least fix the light for all the poor saps that get stuck in here thanks to the stupid bullies. The Junkyard was shaping up to be just as bad as regular school, except the bullies were slightly more sophisticated.

I wouldn't mind sticking Nash in here for a few hours to see how he liked it. But then again I guess he'd get his desserts soon enough…except it'd be his death, and *that* seemed a bit too extreme a punishment.

There had to be a way out.

I stood up and ran my hands over the panel near the door. While the lights were out, I knew there must still be power running through the capsule. Maybe if I could find the wires, I could get lucky.

I grabbed at the console and pulled it, but it stuck tight. I brushed over it with my fingers, feeling for any indents where it might've been screwed on. There were two small indents—one at the top and the other at the bottom. Nuts. It was secured. I could look for a screwdriver in the dark and attempt to remove them, but I had a better, more sophisticated, method.

I bashed the console with my broken flashlight and cracked the plastic covering. After a couple more careful hits, I was able to pull some plastic shards from the console.

I felt some wires behind the casing and realized that I really didn't have much of an idea what I was doing. Maybe there was a failsafe built into the wiring. Maybe if it was shorted out, the door would default to open. Then again, I could just as easily electrocute myself.

I took one of the smooth wires in my hand and pulled out my knife. One quick cut and I would see what would happen. I mean, sure I could die, but surviving the end of the world seemed statistically less probable anyway.

I gritted my teeth and slashed the cord. The good news was that I didn't die. The bad news was that nothing else happened either.

Guess I could try the next wire.

I took it in my hand and closed my eyes.

Vrooom!

My eyes jolted open. Parker stood outside the open door. It worked? Was there was just a delay on the circuits?

"I'm a freaking genius!" I said.

Parker cocked his head and looked at the wires in my hand. "Gage, what are you doing?"

"I figured there might be a failsafe on the door if the wires were cut, and that it would default to being open."

Parker held up a keycard. "Or a buddy could just open the door for you, without the risk of stranding yourself forever."

The wires dropped from my hands. "All due respect, I had no idea you were coming, and since when do you have Level 4 access?"

Parker grinned and bowed. "Ever since I stole it from..." he squinted at the card. "Oscar."

I stepped out of the capsule and kicked the side of it. The stars were bright and the wind was chilly, but it was better than being trapped in that stupid thing. "When'd you have time to steal that thing anyway?" I asked.

"I thought you learned your lesson," Parker said, smiling. "I took it when the officer, Oscar, grabbed me to distract him for you to get into the mirror. I couldn't let a perfect distraction go to waste. So I picked his pocket." Parker grabbed me and turned me from side to side. "So tell me, was the mission successful? What Relic've you got up your sleeve?"

I grabbed Parker's arms, held them at his sides, and shook my head. Parker's brows furrowed. "Let's go. We gotta get Wesley."

Parker's mouth dropped. "Wesley? Why?"

I led Parker away from the broken capsule and toward Wesley's.

"I found something. The Upheavals aren't going to stop. They're gonna get worse. Wesley's the only one who can stop them."

Parker smirked. "You're kidding?"

I shook my head.

"And you're sure Wesley's the only one who can help?"

"That's what the light-girl-computer-thingy said."

"Dude! What are you talking about? Did that mirror thing scramble your brains into mac-n-cheese or what?"

It did sound crazy, but now it was my turn. "I know it sounds nuts, but I *was* a mouse today, remember?"

"And that's supposed to make me believe you more?"

Hmm. Good point. "I'm just saying lots of crazy stuff is possible. You gotta believe me. This is serious."

Parker nodded. "Fine, fine. But why Wesley?"

"The girl-computer said that he took something that allowed her to…keep the Upheavals under control." I decided not to mention the creature living in the center of the world. I mean how much crazy-talk could a guy take before writing me off as certifiably insane?

"Why'd he do that?" Parker asked.

"She said he was hearing voices in his head. I mean I know I just met the guy, but don't you think he's been acting weird?"

"People call him Fido; that should tell you something. Even Tes says he's been acting strange."

Heat singed in my cheeks when he mentioned Tes. What was up with her anyway?

Parker smirked. "Why are you blushing, Gage? You gotta thing for Tes? I'd stay away from her if I were you."

Of course Parker would tell him to back off. He's been shadowing her like a fruit fly. But after what she did, maybe I should back off. "You're right about one thing. We should stay away from her. She and her bonehead boyfriend are the reason I was locked in the capsule in the first place. She sold me out!"

"What? But this whole thing was her idea in the first pla..." Parker shook his head as the realization seemed to fall upon him.

"Exactly, and I'd love to know why she double crossed us, but we have more important problems to be dealing with right now."

"Right," Parker said. "Find Wesley. Speaking of which, there's his capsule over there."

The good news was that Parker was right—we'd made it back to Wesley's capsule. The bad news was that the door to the capsule was already open, someone was there, and worst of all, it wasn't Wesley.

Two men dressed in military camos were scouring through the room, rummaging through books and tinkering with the small devices Wesley had all over.

"Who are those guys?" Parker asked.

He probably didn't mean for me to answer, but I did know who they were. "They're the guys that dropped me off here in the helicopter."

One of them had grey hair and was clean shaven except for a perfectly trimmed white mustache. I never caught his name. The other one I knew—Mr. Russell. He had a younger looking rounded face with dark blond hair.

By the time I'd seen them it was too late to hide. Their focus snapped from Wesley's gadgets to Parker and me.

"What are you two doing here?" Mr. Russell asked, stepping towards us.

"And why are you out so late?" the older one asked, looking down towards his watch.

I looked at Parker for support, but his wide eyes suggested he was as surprised as I was and also didn't know what to say.

"Hey, aren't you the guys from the helicopter?" I asked.

Mr. Russell seized me by the shirt. "Never mind that. Where's the Relic?"

The other man placed his hand on his partner. "Take it easy, Russell. What makes you think these kids know anything?"

Mr. Russell tightened his grip on me. His knuckles dug into my chest. "Let him answer the question."

"If you're talking about the glove, Nash took it from me," I said.

Mr. Russell released me and shoved me back a step. "Glove?" he turned to the older man. "Crane, what's he talking about?"

"Wait," Parker said. "Why are you guys looking for a Relic in Wesley's room?"

"Some kid stole a Relic from Dr. Renner," the older man said, rubbing his mustache. "He'd reportedly stashed it here."

Parker shook his head as if he didn't understand, but now I knew exactly what was going on.

I elbowed Parker. "The distraction, remember?"

"What are you talking about?" Parker whispered.

"You told the officers that you hid a Relic in Wesley's room, remember?"

Parker slapped his forehead and nodded.

"Crane, did you see any glove?" Mr. Russell asked his partner.

"Didn't you hear me?" I asked. "Nash alread—"

"No, nothing like that here," Crane said.

"Does Dr. Renner know you guys are here?" Parker asked.

Mr. Russell and Crane's heads snapped towards Parker. "That's classified. This is all part of an ongoing investigation," Crane said.

Mr. Russell put his hand on Crane's shoulder and whispered, "They don't need to know any of this."

"What's it matter, these kids aren't under suspicion. And from the sounds of it, they'll be leaving here tomorrow anyway," Crane said.

"There's still no point in letting it slip to a couple mischievous kids," Mr. Russell said, inching towards us. "Who still haven't answered what they're doing here at three in the morning."

"We're just looking for Wesley," I said. "He was on our team during the delving expedition. We wanted to talk to him to see if he'd found anything."

Crane scratched his grey hairs. "Expeditions ended hours ago kids. All activities have been put on hold. You should all be in bed."

Parker jumped in. "That's why we're out so late. Look, Gage and I just got here yesterday. We haven't even had a full day to prove ourselves and we're already being told we're being sent home. Can you really blame us for trying to find something before that happens?"

Mr. Russell's face contorted like he's just smelled yesterday's meatloaf, but Crane smiled and nodded his head.

"We have to detain them," Mr. Russell said.

"Why?" Crane asked.

"They're breaking the rules," Mr. Russell said.

"And for all the right reasons," Crane said.

Mr. Russell shook his head. "I don't want it coming down on me."

"They're not gonna tell anyone. And even if they do, I'll take the blame," Crane said.

"There's no compromising on this," Mr. Russell said. "They broke curfew, we *have* to detain them."

"Actually," I said. "According to the Delver's Safety Manual you gave me, searching for a lost team member is a higher priority than curfew."

Mr. Russell stood motionless with his mouth wide open and speechless, just like I remembered him from the helicopter.

Crane covered his mouth, but let out a quick snort.

Mr. Russell's face turned red. "Report to Dr. Renner's office right now!"

"Why?" Parker asked. "It's two o'clock. It's not like he'll even be there."

Crane rushed forward and stood between us and Mr. Russell, whose fists were clenched and was grinding his teeth.

"Dr. Renner is awake and in his office," Crane said. "He's trying to get everything prepared for the changeover tomorrow."

"But we need to find Wesley," I said. "We can't waste our time going to Dr. Renner."

Mr. Russell yelled, "It's not your choice to make. Report to Dr. Renner's office, now!"

Crane faced his partner and put both his hands up. "Cool it, hotshot. These kids aren't doing anything wrong."

Mr. Russell pushed Crane to the side.

"Whoa! Eas—" I started

"Gentlemen," Parker interrupted and reached into his pocket. "There's no need to fight. Mr. Russell's right. We should be detained. But here," Parker pulled a coin from his pocket, "let's leave it to chance. Heads, we surrender to being detained. Tails, we go immediately to Dr. Renner's office and wait for our planes home."

What the heck? "What are you talking about, Parker?" I asked. I could understand being sent to Dr. Renner's office. At least he might have some idea where Wesley was. But being detained meant we would never find Wesley. And leaving it to a coin flip?

"You can't be serious," Mr. Russell said.

71

Crane just laughed. "You gotta give it to these kids, they've got guts."

"What's the problem?" Parker asked. "Both options were your idea anyway."

Mr. Russell crossed his arms.

Crane crouched down to Parker. "You sure you want to do this?"

Parker smiled and nodded, which was the complete opposite of what I was doing at the moment. I couldn't believe it. I was actually on Mr. Russell's side. This was ridiculous!

I shook my head, but Parker just elbowed me.

"Alright then, flip it. But let it fall to the ground," Crane said, bending down to get a closer look. His eyes betrayed his amusement in the whole situation.

Parker flipped the coin.

It clinked on the ground, but I couldn't look.

"Tails it is!" Crane said. I opened my eyes to confirm the good news.

"Ugh," Mr. Russell sputtered. "You can't be serious? This is nonsense. We *have* to detain them. It's our responsibility."

"Let it go, already," Crane slapped Mr. Russell's back. "They're just kids. And they're smart kids with courage and a sense of adventure. They're not criminals."

Mr. Russell pulled what looked like a white string from a metal bar in Wesley's capsule. "Fine. Let's just find the Relic and be done with this stupid job."

Crane approached, knelt down and took the coin. "You two need to get a move on to Dr. Renner's office. It's within viewing distance from here, so don't get any ideas."

Parker held out his hand for the coin. Crane turned it over, shook his head and grinned so big his cheeks rose like tiny hills in front of his eyes. Parker shrugged and his face turned red.

Crane whispered, "double-sided coin, huh?" He dropped the coin in Parker's hand.

Parker nodded. "What are the chances?"

"I hope you find your friend," Crane said.

I hoped to find Wesley too, but there were a lot of strange things going on. Who called these guys in? What were they looking for? And most of all, what happened to Wesley?

CHAPTER 12

CLOSE QUARTERS

Dr. Renner was not only in his office, awake at just before four in the morning, but he wasn't alone. I heard the muffled voices of Nash and Tes inside, too. The door was cracked open, and Parker and I stood just outside, listening to the conversation.

I peeked in through the window.

Dr. Renner's office was decorated with pictures of him shaking hands with old guys in lab coats. There were framed documents, diplomas, and other boring stuff. The only picture with Tes in it was when she looked like she was about ten. She stood beside her father who was showing off some machine.

Dr. Renner shook the glove Nash stole from me. "How's it work?" he asked Nash.

"I don't really know. All I know is it feels really weird when you put your hand in it," Nash answered.

"Then why couldn't this wait until morning?" Dr. Renner asked, tossing it onto his desk, cluttered with papers and files. "Can't you see I'm busy getting all the paperwork in order for the turnover?"

Nash rubbed the back of his neck. "To be fair, Dr. Renner, it *is* morning."

Tes giggled and put her arms around Nash.

Dr. Renner shook his head. So did I. I mean, it wasn't even that funny.

"Tesla, get away from him," Dr. Renner said.

She put her arms on her side. "Why do you get to tell me what to do?"

"Because I run this place," Dr. Renner said.

"We're all leaving tomorrow anyway, so what I guess that doesn't matter anymore," Tes said.

"What?" Nash asked.

"I'm still your dad," Dr. Renner said.

"Wait. What do you mean we're all leaving tomorrow? Is that what you meant by turnover?" Nash asked.

"Mind your own business," Dr. Renner.

Nash stepped towards Dr. Renner. "It sounds like it is my business."

"Your only business is delving for Relics, and we're not doing that right now. So go back to your capsule," Dr. Renner said.

Tes' voice shot in. "Stop being such a jerk, Dad."

I couldn't believe she was sticking up for Nash. Why didn't she stick up for me when he threw me in the capsule? I was the one who risked my life trying to help her. All Nash has done so far is bully me around.

Dr. Renner retrieved the glove from his desk. "You want to help, Tesla? Why don't you tell me where you found this thing?"

Tes looked down, quiet as a mouse.

"What's it matter where we found it?" Nash asked.

Parker pushed past me and opened the door. "They won't tell you, Dr. Renner, because they weren't the ones who found it. Gage was."

All of a sudden, all eyes were on us. Parker entered the office, and I slumped in behind him.

Dr. Renner stood motionless like a statue, obviously confused to see us in his office. But Nash's eyes were even wider. Tes was shocked too, but had a smirk on her face.

"Doesn't anyone sleep around here?" Dr. Renner asked. "What do you mean Gage found this Relic?"

I nodded. "Yes, sir. I found it in a cave in the southern part of camp. Nash stole it from me, then locked me in the broken capsule."

"None of that's true. He just wants to win the event for the Red Team, so he's trying to claim that Relic as his," Nash said. "Besides, his story's obviously a lie. If I locked him in the capsule, then how'd he get out?"

"I let him ou—" Parker started, until I elbowed him in the ribs. "ou...ch"

I didn't want anyone to know that Parker got me out with a stolen keycard.

"There's no need arguing about it," I said, looking at Tes. "Just ask your Tes. She saw Nash put me in there. She knows what happened."

Dr. Renner crossed his arms. "Is this true?"

Tes' eyes were locked on mine. She scratched her nose and slowly shook her head.

"See..." Nash said.

My face flushed with heat. I didn't want to believe that Tes was actually working against me, but it was getting hard to think otherwise. But I guess it didn't really matter now. The glove wasn't what was important; finding Wesley was.

"She's lying," Parker said. "I'm the one who got Gage out of the ca—"

I elbowed Parker again.

Parker whispered, "Stop doing that."

"Don't tell them anything," I whispered back.

"What?" Dr. Renner asked.

"Fine. Whatever. Nash found the stupid glove that he doesn't even know how to use," I blurted out, before Parker admitted to busting me out. "I don't even care about the glove. I just want to know where Wesley is."

Dr. Renner shook his head the second I said Wesley's name and his face went red and he glared at me. "He's asleep in his capsule."

"No, he's not," Parker said. "We were just there."

"That's strange," Dr. Renner said, scratching his nose. "What do you need with Wesley, anyway?"

"We're just worried about him," I said. I don't know why, but I lied to Dr. Renner. Something about the way he was acting reminded me of when Tes lied.

Dr. Renner nodded. "Okay, I didn't want anyone to know. There have been reports of him stealing Relics and hiding them in his room. I had him removed earlier."

Tes shook her head. Did she know something about this?

Parker scratched the back of his head. "No, Dr. Renner, I made all that up. Me and Tes. It was just a—"

"Wait," I said, elbowing Parker. "Did you lock him up or what? Where is he?"

Parker pushed me back. "Stop jabbing me in the side. It's starting to hurt."

I whispered to Parker, "Don't tell him anything. He's lying to us."

Dr. Renner squinted at Parker, as if trying to understand what he was talking about. "That's classified information."

"No," I said. "You don't understand. I need to know where he is. It's really important."

Nash shoved forward and picked me up by the back of my jacket. "Shut it, Mickey. Dr. Renner said he couldn't tell you."

I shook and kicked behind me, but he was too strong. "Let me go, you stupid baboon."

Parker clawed at Nash, but got kicked to the ground.

Tes ran forward and knelt down to help Parker. "Leave him alone," she said. "He didn't do anything."

"Knock it off, all of you," Dr. Renner said. "There'll be no violence in my office."

Great. No violence, just lying and secrets.

Nash tossed me and I cracked my butt on the hard wood floor. Tes knelt down next to me. "You okay?" she asked. Her eyes watered a little, but I didn't have anything to say to her.

"Just leave me alone," I said.

"But I think I can hel—"

"You heard him, get out of here, you liar," Parker said.

"Everyone out," Dr. Renner said. "Get back to your capsules."

Nash stomped near and grabbed Tes' hand. "Come on, let's go."

"Get away from my daughter," Dr. Renner said.

Nash didn't seem to care and pulled Tes away from me.

Tes turned to me and whispered, "I know where Wesley is."

I wanted to wonder whether or not I could trust her or not, but just after she said that, the pulsing Upheaval alarms blared.

"What the…" Nash stuttered.

"Again? Already?" Parker asked, looking towards Dr. Renner.

"We should all be fine here," Dr. Renner said. "We're in the safe-zone."

We were in the safe-zone, but that didn't stop the room from rumbling. Dr. Renner's photos and diplomas toppled to the floor.

I yelled, "The Upheavals are getting stronger."

"Get to your capsules!" Dr. Renner shouted.

I shot up and darted for the door, along with Parker, Nash and Tes.

In about twenty seconds we were outside running towards the capsules, but we hadn't planned on the Upheaval starting in under a minute. The fact that it started early signaled bad things to come. Number one on that list was the fact that we were only halfway to our safety capsules.

The earth rumbled beneath us, then shot us each into the air, like confetti being shot from a funnel. I landed on my back near a fence post. Above me the sky was just beginning to hint at the morning sun. I noted the position of the moon and a bright star I assumed was actually Venus and made them my anchors. Nothing on earth could be counted on to stand still. Even the fence next to me had plummeted into the earth.

I jumped up. There was no sign of Parker, Tes, or Nash. I sprinted in the direction of the capsules.

A screech echoed in the chaotic rumbling from my right. It sounded like Tes. I clenched my fists. Warm blood rushed through my arms and face.

Not again.

I just kept running. There was no time to help.

"Help," she screamed.

The sound of her voice made me stop in my tracks. I had to help her. Not because I liked her. Not because it was the right thing to do...

No, I had to because she knew where Wesley was.

I swiveled right and dashed towards the sound. My foot caught a faulty rock and I tripped as the earth beneath me tumbled down like a runaway elevator. I shouted and caught the ground just above the chasm and held on tight, but my position wasn't good. I dug my feet into the earth, but they kept slipping off.

The pit below was dark. How far it went down, I didn't know. But it was surely too deep for anyone to survive from this height.

"Help!" I shouted.

My hands started to slip, so I dug my fingers into the dirt.

The smell of sweat and apples rippled from above me and something took my wrist.

Above me was Tes. Her face was smudged with dirt and her hair was everywhere, but she never looked better as far as I was concerned.

Tes pulled my arm. "You're going to have to help."

"Right." I balanced my feet on the earth and scrambled up the side.

"Where are the capsules?" she asked, as I got out of the pit.

I located the moon and Venus.

"This way," I shouted, grabbing her arm and bolting.

I tugged at her arm for a short moment, but before I knew it I was the one being tugged. I'd heard girls matured faster than boys, and she was already two years older—her legs carried her far faster than mine did me.

A slab of earth crashed down between us and I lost touch of her hand. Dust shot up from the ground obstructing my view.

"Tes, where are you?" I shouted.

In the rumbling I could barely hear her. "Over here."

I dashed towards her sound. The dust was like a heavy fog, but the faint outline of Tes came into view. A capsule lay at the bottom of a hill. She entered and door began to close behind her. She pressed her hand on the console and the door remained open. Unfortunately, I couldn't stop my sprint and crashed right into her, landing on top of her.

The capsule door slammed shut behind us.

"Sorry," I said.

She pushed me off and pulled me inside the tiny sleeping chamber. It was a tight fit to say the least, and I could feel the warmth of her breath on my lips and nose.

"Don't stare at me like that," she said. "It's weird."

"Sorry," I said, doing my best not to stare at her. "There's just not a whole lot to look at."

I nodded and noticed how tightly our bodies were smooshed together. Her body was so soft and warm. For all I cared, the Upheaval could last for eternity and I'd be happy. Awkwardly happy.

And a little hungry.

"That better not be your hand," Tes said.

Sweat percolated in my armpits. I didn't do it on purpose, but my hand was resting around her waist.

"I'm so, so, so sorry," I said.

"Just move it. And stop apologizing. You did save my life, you know."

"To be fair, you saved mine too," I said.

"And what is that jabbing my leg?" Tes asked.

I forced my hand into my pocket. "Oh, sorry," I said.

"Enough apologizing!"

"It's my king," I said.

"Your what?"

"My chess piece."

She rubbed against me, probably trying to get into a more comfortable position.

"The thing Parker stole?"

"Yup."

Beep. Beep. Beeeeeep

"Figures," Tes said.

"What?" I asked.

"The second we get to safety, the sensor says it's safe to get out."

Figures indeed…that was the shortest eternity ever.

The lid on the sleeping chamber opened from the side and we both toppled over. It seemed the capsule had flipped over on its side during the Upheaval.

"So what's with the chess piece?" Tes said, staggering up and flinging her hair behind her face.

I pulled the king out of my pocket. "I know it's dumb, but chess is my favorite game."

"Why?'

"Because when you're playing, no one is allowed to tell you what to do," I said.

Tes bent down to pick up her shoe, which must've fallen off when we fell from the chamber.

"Um, don't be mad," I said, but you have some dirt on your butt."

She turned her head to see. "Who cares? You should see how dirty you are."

Actually, that was the problem, I must've muddied up my hands pretty bad clawing up the cliff. "It's not just dirty, it's in the shape of my hand."

Tes' faced me and blushed. "Not a word of that to Nash," she said, dusting her butt off.

"Like I'd tell anything to the lying gorilla."

She smiled, which surprised me a little. "And what does that make me?"

"Well, you lied too, but you're not a gorilla."

"I guess I'm a wolf," she said, eyebrows furrowed.

UPHEAVAL

"And I'm a mouse. What's it matter? You may have lied, but at least you made it up to me by saving my life."

She walked close and took my hands, pulling me to my feet. "Well, you came back for me even after I'd lied. I appreciate that kind of loyalty."

Tes' hands were warm. It made me kind of wish another Upheaval would happen.

Tes smiled at me.

My faith in her grew, but it still bothered me that she didn't stick up for me in front of Dr. Renner. "Why did you lie anyway?"

She turned and placed her hand on the sensor. The capsule's side door, now directly above us, opened up letting in a hint of sunlight and clouds of dust.

"It's kinda hard to explain," she finally said, still looking away from me.

"Well if anyone deserves to know, it's gotta be me, right?"

She nodded, folding her hands together and lowering them near the ground to hoist me up out of the opening above us.

"I guess so…" she said. "It's just that I don't like talking about it."

"Talking about what?" I asked, stepping into her hands. "Are you afraid I'd tell someone else?"

"No, nothing like that," she said. "I just don't share things a lot."

"Well, we did share a capsule, didn't we?" I asked.

She giggled a little. The dirt on her cheeks made her look even cuter when she smiled.

She lifted me up and I grabbed hold of the opening, hoisting my body over. She reached up to me and I pulled her out.

"I just don't want Nash to be mad at me," she said.

"Why do you care if he gets mad? He's kind of a jerk."

Her eyes were wet and she clenched her hands and cleared her throat. "I know he can be, but he's not to me. I hate it when he's mean to others. Sometimes I don't even like him that much."

"That makes two of us," I said.

"But other times he'd do anything for me."

"You mean like beat me up and throw me in a broken capsule?" I asked.

Tes crossed her arms. "I know…I'm sorry about that."

"You should get rid of him. He's not worth your time."

Tes shook her head and swallowed. "I think part of it is that my dad can't stand him."

What? Her words were as confusing as the dusty landscape around us—random slabs of earth obscured by clouds of dirt.

"Is that why you protected him in front of your dad? You were just trying to get your dad to like him more?"

Tes laughed a nervous sounding giggle. "My dad'll never like him, no matter what I say."

"Then why lie for him to your dad?"

"Because Dad only cares about me when he's around."

"But you said he doesn't even like Nash."

Tes rubbed her eyes and sighed. Apparently I wasn't understanding her. "Exactly. He's so busy with Wesley all the time, he ignores me, except when Nash's around."

For a second I thought I understood what was going on, until she mentioned Wesley. "What's Wesley have to do with any of this?"

Tes threw her arms to her side. "Never mind. You wouldn't understand."

It felt like she just punched me in the stomach. "Well excuse me for caring."

The dust settled around us in silence. We began walking over the rubble.

"Why are you looking for Wesley anyway?" Tes asked.

I motioned in front of us. "Look around."

The earth looked like it'd been trampled by a thousand-ton crash of rhinos.

Tes shook her head after observing the destruction. "What do you mean?"

"This is what the whole world will be like unless we get Wesley," I said.

"What do you mean?"

"The Upheavals are getting worse. This one hit the safe-zone. The perimeter is widening. It even started before the warning ended. Soon they'll be catastrophic."

"But what's Wesley supposed to do?"

"Never mind, you wouldn't understand." I took her hand. "Let's hurry."

I took off, but she didn't budge. She stared at me and I had seen the way she was staring at me before. It was the same as when I failed to pull the boulder off of her when we first met—if stares could kill, I'd have been dead twice now.

"Do you really want to know why I lied for Nash? Do you really want to know why I'm here at all?"

I released her hand.

Tes sighed. "I could do anything I want and nobody cares. No one even knew that I went out exploring yesterday, until you found me. My dad certainly didn't care. He couldn't care less what I do."

There were tears fighting for control of Tes' eyes, but she breathed deep through her nose to hold them back. I had to admit I couldn't understand her. "That kind of freedom sounds like heaven to me. I wished my parents loosened up like that. They're always telling me what to do. That's why *I'm* here."

Tes brushed her hair back behind her ear. "It's not at all as nice as you think. Dad didn't care at all…until Nash showed up. Nash always wanted me to be on his team and we'd go for walks after hours. It made my dad furious. He got so mad he banned us from being on the same team. But we would still go on walks after hours. He made me feel special."

I guess I felt a little bad for her, but it was hard. Maybe Nash made her feel special, but he made me feel like trash. "So that's why you didn't stick up for me?"

Tes sighed. "I'm sorry. It's just hard for me. Nash makes me feel good…and it makes my dad crazy, too."

"I don't get it. Why do you want to make Dr. Renner mad?"

"Because at least when Nash is around, he acknowledges that I exist. I've spent years memorizing all this stupid science stuff to make him happy. Except now…"

"Except what?"

"Now all he cares about is Wesley."

"Wesley? What's he care about him for?"

Tes sighed, pulled my hand, and began walking. "I'm not sure, but he's at campus."

"How'd you know that?"

"He's been working with my dad for a while now. Whenever we go on delving expeditions, Wesley finds some excuse to leave. Dad takes him back to campus to work on his top-secret stuff."

I took Tes' hand. "Well, let's go get him."

"We'll have to find a helicopter," Tes said, following behind me.

We climbed over a clearing. The safe-zone looked like it'd been chomped up and spit out by giants.

"A helicopter…" I said. "Even if we found one, who'd fly it for us?"

Tes said nothing and walked past me. I picked up my pace. The sun outlined the horizon with a golden string, but there was also a faint light amongst the rocks. It looked like a capsule.

"I guess I could figure it out. I mean, how hard could flying a helicopter be?" I asked.

Tes shook her head and snorted. "Even if you had Level 4 access to open the Helicapsule door, you'd never stand a chance flying it safely without weeks of training."

"Level 4 access is no problem" I said. "The weeks of training part, though...well, hopefully there's an autopilot." I laughed.

We approached near the capsule. Its light faded off.

Tes laughed too. "Well, I'm pretty sure that's not how helicopters work. And I'm very sure I would not get into a helicopter with *you* as the pilot."

Honestly, I wouldn't want to be in a helicopter with me either. One thing for sure is that I'd have to find Parker first, and hope he still had the stolen card.

"Isn't there any other way to get out of here?" I asked.

Tes shook her head. "Trains were shut down long ago. The Upheavals made land-based travel impractical. Helicopters are the only way these days."

An older man's voice cut in, "What do you need a helicopter for?"

Crane inched out of the capsule, holding his shoulder and wincing. "And where's the other kid...the one with the coin?" Crane asked.

"We're looking for him," I said. "But we lost contact with him in the Uphea—"

Tes scooted in front of me, as if to protect me. "And who're you?"

Crane grunted and clenched his fists. "Sorry about that." He outstretched his hand offering a handshake and revealed that his shoulder was pierced with some stony shrapnel. "Adam Crane. Mark Russell and I are here investigating alleged wrongdoing."

Tes shook his hand.

"Where's your partner?" I asked.

"The Upheaval took us by surprise, and we got separated in the chaos," Crane said. "I'd be looking for him, but I need to get my shoulder checked out, and fast."

"They can treat that back at campus," Tes said.

"I'm a little disoriented," Crane said, shaking his head. "Could you lead the way?"

"Sure," I said. "Where's your helicopter?"

"In a Helicapsule about half-a-mile east of the Administration Building, or whatever's left of it." Crane said.

"That's assuming the Upheaval's perimeter hasn't increased too much," Tes said.

"The Helicapsule should keep it safe," Crane said. "Although, if it's buried it won't be of much use to us."

"We need to get back to campus, too," I said. "Any chance you would take us with you?"

Crane stifled a smile. "Of course you can come. If I start to lose consciousness, I'll need you to fly it for me."

"You have to be kidding," Tes said.

CHAPTER 13

DESERTION

The good news was that I didn't have to try to fly the helicopter. And Tes was right—Wesley *was* on campus working for Dr. Renner. The bad news was Dr. Renner was there too, which would make getting Wesley out of there much harder.

We made a quick trip to the medical center. Crane had lost a lot of use in his left arm, but was able to secure for himself a generous amount of liquid painkillers. Injected right into the bloodstream via syringe, Crane felt much better, but it made Tes' face drain of all color. I guess she wasn't a big fan of needles.

Normally we wouldn't have been able to get into Dr. Renner's lab, but Crane had access, and if he had any problems with us tagging along, he didn't show it.

The lab was clustered with Relics all over the place. Broken shards and half-finished machinery were cluttered on the tables around the corners. Some items were mounted on the maroon walls next to photos of scientists at work, but it was the table that Wesley worked at that was most interesting. Vials of colored compounds, burners, and machinery littered the long black table. In front of Wesley was the glove I'd been given as well as a rounded device about the size of a shoe.

Dr. Renner's face was a mix of confusion and anger when he saw us. "Get out of here!" he yelled. "This is a restricted area."

Wesley looked up from his work. His lips curled up in a small smile, but he narrowed his eyes on me.

Crane produced his name badge with his good hand. "I'm Adam Crane. I've been commissioned to investigate some reported violations of the safety procedures here. Mind if I look around?" he asked, examining items on the wall not at all waiting for permission.

"I wasn't notified about this," Dr. Renner said.

"That's because you're one of the persons we're investigating," Crane said.

"That's ridiculous," Dr. Renner said.

"Wesley," I said. "You gotta come with us."

"He's not going anywhere with you," Dr. Renner said. "He's busy here. Besides, even if Mr. Crane has business here, *you* certainly have no right to be in here."

"Chill out Dad," Tes said. "We just need to talk to Wesley for a little."

"Get out of here," Dr. Renner said, crossing his arms. "This is a place for real scientists."

"Nice to see you too, Dad. Glad to see you're happy I'm alive after that Upheaval nearly killed me."

Dr. Renner's eyes widened for a moment, but his face hardened again. "I'm glad you're okay, now get out!"

"But if we leave now," I interjected, "I won't be able to show you how the glove works."

"What're you talking about? Why didn't you say anything about that before?" Dr. Renner asked.

Crane ceased examining the Relics and shards on the walls and turned to pay close attention to the conversation.

"What's it matter? I can show you how the glove works, but you have to let Wesley leave with us if I do."

Dr. Renner placed his hand on Wesley's shoulder. "You make it sound like he's a prisoner or something. He's here working with me because he wants to. You don't just get to barge in here making accusations...or deals."

"Dad, you're being unfair. Gage is just trying to help," Tes said. "Wesley, Gage and I have a big problem and we really need your help. Can you help us?"

Wesley didn't seem to even hear the question. His eyes were on Crane the whole time.

"Tesla, we're very busy in here," Dr. Renner said. "Wesley might have unlocked the secret behind the Upheavals. We don't have time to worry about your problems."

By the way Tes' face went red and teary-eyed, you'd have thought Dr. Renner'd just told her that she was adopted. Then again, she probably would've welcomed news like that better.

"He's impossible, Gage. Let's get out of here," Tes said, choking back her tears.

I couldn't leave. Tes was upset, but I had to ignore her for the moment. I moved towards the table. "Has Wesley figured out how to activate the glove?"

Dr. Renner's eyebrows furrowed and he tilted his head towards Wesley. "Well Wesley, have you?"

Wesley glared at me. "It doesn't matter. It's just a piece of junk."

"He's wrong," I said. "For all you know, it could be the most important Relic we've discovered. And I know how to use it."

"Dr. Renner, don't listen to him. He doesn't kno—"

"Enough, Wesley!" He said, sliding the glove towards me. "Show me."

"Promise to let Wesley come with us?" I asked.

"Impress me first, then we'll talk," Dr. Renner said.

I grabbed the edge of the table, and shook it a little. It was really heavy. "What's this table made from?"

"It's granite," Tes said.

"Is it bolted to the ground?" I asked.

Dr. Renner's head tilted. "No. Why?"

I took the glove and put it on. I withdrew the light-pen from my pocked and slid it into a groove in the glove.

"What's that?" Wesley asked.

"Watch," I said, sliding up the light fader illuminating the glove.

I grabbed the desk and pushed.

Nothing happened.

"Stop wasting time," Wesley said.

"I'm not wasting time," I said. "I wanted to demonstrate that while the glove is inactive, it doesn't do anything, but when it's activated…"

I slid up the second fader on the light-pen and the desk's material oscillated and moved easily under the little pressure I provided.

Dr. Renner jumped back and let out an audible, "Whoa!"

I only barely heard Dr. Renner though. The moment I pushed up the second fader Wesley started screaming and grabbing at the back of his neck.

"Earbuds!" Wesley yelled. His eyes were wide and crazed like he'd been beaten with a stick. He thrashed towards the desk, flinging vials and Relics towards me.

I jumped back removing my grasp from the desk.

Wesley smashed his hands onto the desk and propelled himself over it, charging at me. His eyes were fiery with pain. He shrieked as if being tortured.

"Whoa! It's okay," I said putting my hands up.

But it didn't matter at all to Wesley.

He smashed into me and grabbed at the glove.

Tes seized him by the back, but Wesley thrashed at her, flinging her to the ground.

I squirmed and kicked, but his legs pinned me like a metal vise. I grabbed his face and pushed, but he swatted my hand away as easily as a windshield wiper flings water.

He grabbed the glove with both hands and ejected my light-pen from its casing.

Then he went silent. His wide eyes sagged a bit, losing their focus and drifting off towards nothing in particular. His plier-like grip on me relaxed.

Crane gently pushed Wesley's shoulder and he collapsed off of me like a bowling pin, almost with a smile on his face.

Then I saw why. Crane held an emptied syringe in the air. He must've injected Wesley with enough painkillers to make a deer in a bear-trap feel like she could run a marathon.

"What happened to Wesley? Why'd he go berserk?" I asked.

Tes shook her head, as did Crane.

Dr. Renner may have been the only one who could answer that question. Besides a picture of Dr. Renner with some guys in white lab coats hanging on the wall, there was no sign of Dr. Renner anywhere.

"Where's Dr. Renner?" I asked.

"What?" Crane said, jumping to his feet.

"Dad?" Tes asked.

Crane ran to the door, but shook his head after peering down the hallway. "He must've used Wesley as a distraction to get away."

"You think Dad did that to Wesley?" Tes asked.

"I don't think so," I said. "It happened right when I used the glove."

Crane searched the area. Maybe he thought Dr. Renner was just hiding somewhere.

Tes offered me a hand and I stood up. Together we lifted Wesley to his feet as well. With the painkillers in his system, his legs were just like his brain—bendy and unsure.

"Well, Dr. Renner's gone, but at least we have Wesley and can head back to the Junkyard," I said.

"So long as Crane is willing to take us," Tes said.

Crane frowned, his eyes still surveying the room. "It's gone. He took it."

"What'd he take?" Tes asked.

"The device Wesley was working on," Crane said. He walked to us and put his hand on Wesley's back. "How do you feel?"

Wesley smiled. "I feel it in my ears."

"In your ears?" I repeated.

Wesley nodded his head clumsily. "It's okay, she's gone now."

"Well, that's a relief," Crane said. "You two take care of him while I find Dr. Renner. He'll probably be a little loopy for a few hours. He might feel sick after that."

"You can't leave him like this," Tes said.

"He's in no real danger," Crane said.

"But you can't leave," I said. "We need you to fly us back to the Junkyard."

He shook his head. "Sorry, but Dr. Renner running away is suspicious. I need to find him."

I looked to Tes for help. She had lines of worry scribbled lightly on her forehead. I mouthed the word, "please," and she slowly nodded.

"There's no rush," Tes said. "I'm his daughter and I know where he's going."

"Really?" Crane said. "How can you be so sure?"

"You said so yourself. He took the device. He's going back to the Junkyard to complete his project."

"Project?" Crane asked.

I wondered the same thing myself. What was she talking about?

"I'm not sure what it is," Tes said. "But he's been working with Wesley on it for a while."

"Is this true?" Crane asked Wesley.

He nodded clumsily.

"You're sure he's going to the Junkyard?" Crane asked.

"No doubt in my mind," Tes said.

"Dr. Renner's not going to like what'll happen to him when he gets there either," Wesley said.

CHAPTER 14

MORE BAD NEWS

Carrying Wesley I knew what a turtle must've felt like. That is, if the turtle's shell was made of a big, heavy, sweaty teenager.

My legs shook under his weight. Tes was of little help as she walked with Crane who, "couldn't be burdened while tracking a potentially dangerous suspect." Then again, I couldn't really blame him either. He did take a pretty big hit to his shoulder during the last Upheaval.

Tes led Crane towards the cave, doing her best to convince him that it was the location Dr. Renner was heading to.

Crane yelled at us to hurry up every now and again, but it's not like yelling magically made Wesley weigh less. The only good thing about the whole situation was that Wesley was so loopy that it was kind of fun talking to him.

"He thinks he's so smart," Wesley said. "But he's got no idea."

"Who's got no idea?" I asked.

"Dr. Renn..." he stammered. "He's blind as a Texas Salamander."

"What do you mean?" I asked.

"He thinks I'm working with him, but I'm the one who called...wait, um, I think it's a secret."

"C'mon," I said. "I'm helping you out aren't I? You can trust me. I trusted you."

Wesley giggled. "Yeah...you're helping me. He's so dumb." He shook his head. "He gives me anything I want."

"Like what?" I asked.

"He wants me to figure out how the metal works. He was even willing to get explosives for me."

I nearly crumbled under the weight, not of Wesley, but of the thought of Wesley with explosives.

"Explosives?"

Wesley lifted a finger to his lips. "Shh...that's a secret."

"What do you need them for?" I asked.

"It's all part of the plan," Wesley said.

"Does your plan involve hurting people?" I asked.

Wesley laughed. "Dr. Renner said the same thing. Nobody believes me around here. I told him I needed it to test the metal."

"Did it work? Did you figure out how it worked?" I asked.

"It's so simple a dog would know. It all comes down to vibrations," Wesley said. "But Dr. Renner didn't care about that..." Wesley's voice harshened. I could feel his muscles tense on my shoulder. "Maybe he'd care if she did it to him, too."

"Did what to him?" I asked.

"But he got me everything I needed to fix that," he said, smiling again.

"Fix what?" I asked.

"Can't he walk any better by himself yet?" Crane called back to us.

Wesley giggled. "He'll find out everything he's been up to."

I slipped Wesley's hand over my head to let him try to walk by himself. "Whose gonna find out everything?" I asked.

Wesley waddled like an infant taking his first steps, then toppled to the ground. I pulled him up. "Try again," I said.

He staggered forward a couple steps before losing balance. I caught him by his arm. It seemed to work okay. It was better than having him hunched over me, anyway.

"Sorry to repeat myself," I said. "But who's gonna find out everything?"

"*He* is," Wesley said, nodding at Crane. "I didn't expect him to be here so soon, though..." he trailed off, his eyes squinting.

"Crane's here too soon?" I asked. "Too soon for what?"

"I have a plan to fix everything and then they'll know."

Figuring out *who* Wesley was talking about was just as hard as figuring out *what* he was talking about. I wondered if it even made sense to him.

Before long we were underneath the earth in the sloping cave. Cold wind whipped my face and arms. Wesley shivered too, and it seemed to make him more alert.

"Wait...we shouldn't be here yet," Wesley said. "I don't have my earbuds." He started pulling back.

While the painkillers seemed to be fading, he still wasn't making much sense.

"Now's not the time to be worried about music," I said.

Wesley slowed and held his head, like he was trying to remember something. "I can't be here without my earbuds."

"It's okay," I said, pulling his arm.

Wesley resisted me. "No, it's not. I configured them for this moment. I need them."

"Tes' got them, c'mon," I lied, leading him forward.

"Good," Wesley said. "I'm gonna need those."

Crane spoke back to me, "Tes says we're getting close. Is this the right place?"

It was. We were nearly there. Crane wouldn't be happy when he found out that Dr. Renner wasn't there, but once he saw the woman made of light, I was sure he'd understand.

"Almost," I said. "Just a little further."

"What's Dr. Renner trying to do down here anyway?" Crane asked.

"He's got no idea what's going on down here," Wesley interrupted.

"And what's that?" Crane asked.

"The end of the world," Wesley said. "She'll be powerless soon enough."

Tes glanced back at Wesley and I. "What's he talking about? The end of the world?"

Funny enough, that was the first thing Wesley had said that I actually understood. He was wrong though—Kat wouldn't be powerless once I brought Wesley here. He'd be able to help her save the world.

"The world's not ending on my watch," I said.

"What are you two talking about?" Crane asked. "What's Dr. Renner planning to do down here?"

Wesley's muscles tightened and his fists clenched. "I just told you!" Wesley shouted. "He's got no idea what's going on down here. He's too involved in trying to make a name for himself. He's almost as bad as she is."

"She?" Crane asked. "Who are you talking about?"

The tunnel to the cave opened to the metallic room. The Barrix lined the walls and the ceiling glowed dimly.

Wesley broke free from me and ran to Tes. He grabbed her by the jacket. "Give me my earbuds," he said.

Tes shoved Wesley away. He staggered back and fell on his butt. He shot an angry glance at me.

"You said she had the earbuds," Wesley said.

"I don't even know what the heck you're talking about," I said. "You're delusional from the painkillers."

Wesley jumped at Tes, knocking her to the ground. She screamed when Wesley fell on her leg.

"Where are they?" Wesley asked, clawing at her jacket pockets.

Crane pulled Wesley from Tes and stood between them, grasping Wesley's jacket to prevent any further attack. "Knock it off," he said. "Now's not the time to worry about stupid things. We need to—"

The light from the ceiling flashed like lightning. My heart stopped for a brief moment after nearly jumping out of my mouth.

Wesley screamed.

"What's going on?" Crane asked.

Through the veil of light I saw her. She smiled at me.

"It's Kat," I said. "We've done it!"

"You idiot!" Wesley screamed, falling to the ground, holding his ears.

Crane ran to Wesley and bent down to help him.

"Thank you for your help, little mouse," Kat said to me.

Tes pushed herself up. She rubbed her calf. "What the heck is that?"

"That's Kat. She needs Wesley to help her stop the Upheavals from destroying the world."

Wesley pushed Crane away. "She's not trying to help anyone! She's the one waking the creature up."

"Creature…" Tes said. "What creature?"

I shook my head. "No, she said you have something that will help her keep the creature asleep."

Tes crept close to me. "What are you talking about?"

"I'm so happy you came back to be with me," Kat said, looking towards Wesley. Their eyes locked momentarily, then Wesley groaned and began beating his fists into the ground.

"No…no…no…" Wesley stammered.

"Kat, you said you'd persuade him to help you," I said.

Kat smirked. "Don't worry, I'm convincing him right now."

Wesley pushed himself up. His face was pained. He walked towards the console and took a small pin in his hand.

"What's going on here?" Crane asked.

Kat motioned him to draw near to her. "Let me tell you the secret about the Upheavals."

Crane crouched near to her.

"The creature needs help to remake the world," Kat said.

"The creature?" Crane asked.

"And you'll make a great start," she said.

Wesley dashed towards Crane's back, lunged, and pierced the pin into his neck. Crane arched his back and flung Wesley to the side.

I yelled at Wesley. "Stop! What're you doing?"

Crane collapsed to the metal floor, his body convulsing.

"Did you kill him?" I asked.

Wesley turned his gaze at Tes and me.

"What'd you do to him?" Tes asked.

"He's now works for a greater mind," Kat said, smirking. "Just as you will be."

Crane stood up. He ground his teeth and clenched his fists. Like Wesley had, Crane ambled to the console and took two pins.

I tugged at Tes' hand, and ran.

She followed after me.

Unfortunately, Crane wasn't far behind.

"C'mon," I yelled. "Hurry!"

Tes stumbled and crashed to the ground. "I can't, my leg's hurt. Help me."

How was I supposed to help? I was too weak to carry her. I turned and hesitated, staring dumbly, like a deer on a night road.

Crane drew closer to her.

"Carry me," Tes said.

There was no way I could do that for her. Then again, I didn't want her to get stuck with one of those pins in her neck either. So I ran over and tried. I pulled at her to lift her up, but just like when we first met, my strength failed.

"Use the glove!" she said.

"I don't know what it will do," I said.

"Just do it!" she yelled.

I slid on the glove, and inserted the pen. I pushed the faders forward.

Crane's face contorted and went red. He stumbled a second, but continued towards us. Even with his small hesitation, he was close.

He grabbed Tes' hand and flipped her over. Her face hit the ground. He drove the pin at the back of her neck.

I grabbed her by the ankle with the glove and sprinted off.

It felt like I was carrying nothing at all. I hoped that it was because of the glove.

I passed through the entrance, ran and clawed my way out of the dark cave. As soon as the boundless outside air entered my nostrils I looked back for the first time. Crane stood motionless at the entrance of the cave, as if an invisible boundary stopped him. He held his face and shook all over.

The weird thing was that he was at a complete stop. Why wasn't he following me anymore?

I exhaled a long breath and released my grip—Tes lay on the ground behind me, curled up like a shrimp.

She shivered and coughed into the dirt.

I knelt down to help her, but she pushed me away. She held out her hand, telling me to leave her alone a moment.

Crane still stood there, motionless. It creeped me out and I really wanted to leave, but I wasn't about to go without Tes.

Finally, she staggered to her feet.

"C'mon," I said, and she allowed me to help her shamble away arm in arm.

"What happened in there?" Tes asked.

"Kat lied to me," I said. "She used me to get Wesley for her."

"Why?"

"She told me he took something, but I don't know what's true anymore."

"What happened to Crane? Why'd he attack us and stop at the entrance like that?" Tes asked.

"I don't know," I said. "But that pin messed him up pretty bad."

Tes nodded and the wind blew her hair. The tips of her hair tickled my neck and made me forget how angry I was for being manipulated by Kat.

"Thanks for saving me," Tes said, with a small smile.

I nodded and smiled back, but was too embarrassed to look at her eyes. My vision rested elsewhere.

Her leg was bruised from Wesley's attack earlier, and while she needed help walking, its strength seemed to be getting better as we went. It probably didn't feel great, but I bet the glove hurt a lot more.

"What'd it feel like…the glove?" I asked.

She shook her head. "Let's just say next time I'm about to be stabbed by a homicidal maniac, don't use the glove." She smirked.

"Gotcha. Getting stabbed in the back of the neck and being made into a crazed lunatic is better than having all your atoms flickered out of existence."

Tes frowned.

"I was just kidding," I said.

"I know. It's just...we have to do something to help Wesley and Crane. We can't just leave them like that."

"We have bigger problems if what Wesley said is true. If Kat really is using him to wake up the creature, getting stabbed with one of those pins will be nothing compared to what will happen."

Tes pulled away from me and hobbled along alone. "What's all this talk about a creature? You and Wesley both mentioned it."

"There's a creature that lives in the earth. It's where everything comes from. When it dreams, it gives off life into the world."

She stopped in her tracks and placed her hands on her hips. "That's ridiculous!"

My face heated with embarrassment, maybe defensiveness? "I know it sounds crazy. That's why I didn't say anything about it before."

She crossed her arms and crinkled her nose. "Suppose there is this creature. What does it have to do with the Upheavals?"

"Whenever it wakes up, it causes the earth to destroy itself with Upheavals, then it falls back to sleep again. That's what the Relics we're finding are—technology from a previous eon, buried deep from a previous Upheaval."

Tes' eyes widened and her mouth hung lightly ajar. "Does that mean..." Her words drifted off as if she didn't want to finish.

I nodded. "It's waking up."

"I can't believe it," Tes said.

"I know, it was hard for me to belie—"

"No, I mean, Wesley was right!" she said.

"About what?"

"He told me that he was going to put an end to the Upheavals once and for all."

It was my turn to have my mouth hang open stupidly. "Why didn't you say anything before?"

"I thought it was just Wesley being crazy. He told after he'd come back from being missing a week. Everyone thought he was nuts and he stopped talking about it, so I didn't think much of it."

It was starting to make sense to me. Wesley had been in the cave before. He'd met Kat. I'd bet he was the one who blocked off the cave with the stone rubble. Like the last piece of a Rubik's cube coming into place it all made sense to me now. "Where was he delving when he got lost?" I asked.

The cube clicked into place for her too. She nodded. "Here…"

"Kat must've somehow gotten one of those pins in him. That's why he's always wearing hoodies. He was trying to hide the pin in his neck."

"But why hide it?" Tes asked.

"I think he was trying to keep it a secret, so that he could fix the problem," I said.

"But why not ask for help?" Tes asked.

"He doesn't trust anyone," I said. "Maybe he was afraid someone would try to exploit Kat's power and end up causing more harm than good."

"I should've trusted him," Tes said. "And now Crane has one of those pins in his neck, too."

"And she wants to do the same thing to us," I said.

Do you know how they work?" Tes asked.

"Besides making you go crazy, I'm not sure...but both times right before Wesley went berserk he mentioned earbuds. Do you have any idea what he's talking about?"

Tes shook her head.

The earbuds must've been important for something, but I just didn't have enough information to make any sense of it.

"You said Wesley had a plan to solve the problem of the Upheavals, right?" I asked.

"Sure, but I didn't believe him, so he didn't tell me anything." Tes' fingers coiled into fists.

"It's not your fault," I said. "I wouldn't have believed him either. But we need to find someone he may've talked to. Do you know of anyone he was close to?"

Tes let out a grunt of disgust like she'd just stepped in fresh dog poo.

"What?"

"No one believed Wesley, except..." she trailed off.

"Except who?"

She crossed her arms. "Except my dad."

"He knows about all this?" I asked.

Tes bit her lower lip. "I don't think so. It's not that he really believed Wesley, but he did really respect his expertise with the Relics. He just wanted Wesley to figure out how they worked. He'd say anything Wesley wanted to hear. Dad only cares about getting out of here."

"Getting out of here? Why?"

"He views running the Junkyard as a punishment."

"A punishment for what?"

Tes rubbed her face. "Dad's always been fixated on science," she said. Her eyes looked a little moist. "But things didn't work out for him. He wanted to be like his great heroes and revolutionize science."

"And now he's working here…" I said.

Tes shook her head and crossed her arms. "When he failed to make any big discoveries, he set his sights on me. He thought I could be the next great thing to happen in science. I think he's always wanted that."

"I know how you feel. My parents are always trying to control what I do and where I go," I said. "So what happened with you? Did you discover anything amazing?" I asked.

"You don't know what it's like. I tried to live up to his hopes," she said, starting to tear up. "I mean, I just wanted to make him happy. But I just couldn't."

Tes was really upset, I could tell. But unfortunately, I didn't really know how to comfort her. So I just hugged her.

It didn't take long for her sniffles to cease and she wiped her eyes and whispered, "Sorry about that…thank you."

I folded my hands, unsure of how to break the bad news to Tes.

"We need his help, don't we?" Tes asked.

She was no dummy. She knew what we needed to do. "Well, I don't know that he'll be much help to us," I said. "But he's the best shot we have to help Wesley and stop the Upheavals."

Tes sighed and nodded. She waved me forward. "Follow me."

"You know where he is?"

"I've gotta hunch."

CHAPTER 15

EXTRACTION

Dr. Renner must've known something important. He escaped with but one Relic when he disappeared from his office. And now, according to Tes' hunch, he was heading to the capsule that Wesley apparently had private access to—at least he *did*, until Parker and I ran into Crane and Russell searching it out.

And that just made it all the more likely something important was going on. But what?

"Any idea what Wesley was up to?" I asked.

"I was trying to figure that out myself," Tes said, struggling to climb up a particularly steep mount of rock. "Until…"

I took her hand and hoisted her up. "Until what?"

"You know," she said, nodding at her leg.

The Upheaval I rescued her from on the first day. "So that's what you were doing over there."

She smirked. "Didn't go so well."

Maybe it didn't go so well for her, but I was still kind of glad it happened. Otherwise we may not have gotten to know each other at all. I know it was selfish, but who knows, maybe she was a little glad too. But then again, almost dying may have ruined it for her.

"What were you doing out there alone, anyway?" I asked.

"I didn't want anyone knowing what I was up to," she said.

We continued on until we heard a distant familiar voice. "Hello? Anyone out there?"

It was great to hear Parker's voice again. "Hello?" I asked.

"Parker?" Tes asked with a huge smile.

"Gage, Tes! Break a leg and get over here. We've got a big problem."

We tumbled along as fast as Tes' bruised leg could manage, which was actually pretty darned fast.

Parker's face was smudged with dirt. His clothes were ripped up and he was quite messy, but he walked just fine and didn't have any blood on him—just a couple bruises on his arms.

"Are you alright?" Tes asked, caressing his head like a puppy. "Did you make it to a capsule?"

If Parker looked like that, the likelihood of him making it to a capsule was about as good as Wesley not getting picked on by Nash.

"I tried, but I got knocked down. When I got up again, everything was chaos. I couldn't find either of you guys. But I heard a voice through all the noise, so I ran to it," Parker said.

"Whose voice?" Tes asked.

"Nash's. That's why I need your help. He's stuck in the rocks down there," Parker said, motioning with his hands. "I can't get him out."

"Oh my God!" Tes said, grabbing Parker's shoulders. He winced a little. "Is he okay?"

"He's fine, but he's stuck in place. The whole place could collapse any minute, so we gotta hurry. C'mon."

We jogged with Parker along the rocky terrain.

"Down there," he said, scaling down a steep cliff.

"helloooo...Parker?" Nash's voice rebounded off the deep cliff rocks.

"Sounds like he's really far down there," Tes said. Her voice quivered, and for some reason it bothered me. I don't know why, but her concern for Nash made me feel less special.

"Yeah, we dropped pretty far during the Upheaval," Parker said. "We've been keeping each other company for a few hours now. Thank God we found you."

"We don't have time for this," I said. "We have bigger things to worry about right now."

"Knock it off, Gage," Tes said. "We have to help him."

"I have to find Dr. Renner," I said.

Tes grabbed the rope that Parker had anchored. "Then find him. I'm going to help Nash."

"But I need your help," I said.

"So does Nash," Tes said.

Unfortunately, Tes was the one who knew where Dr. Renner was. I'd have to stick close for now, and hopefully this rescue mission wouldn't take long. "Fine. Let's get this over with."

We repelled down the rocks. Tes took the lead and Parker and I followed after.

"What's that on Tes' butt?" Parker asked me.

"You wouldn't believe me if I told you," I said.

"It looks like a hand mark," Parker said.

Tes was pretty far below us by now.

"Let's just say we spent some time in a sleeping chamber together," I said.

Parker's eyes widened. "No way!"

When we were near the bottom, the light from above faded.

"I'm here," Parker shouted to Nash. "And I've got help. We'll be able to get you out of here soon."

When we finally got solid ground under our feet, I gave Parker a little shove and a look like, *why are you so chummy with Nash?*

Parker shrugged. "When it comes to life and death, even bullies are human."

Whatever. Parker didn't have Nash shove him through a mirror that could've killed him or lock him inside a broken capsule after stealing from him. In fact, what did I owe this stupid jerk, anyway? I mean, sure I didn't want him to die or anything, but who knows how long we'd have before Kat started causing even bigger Upheavals? I had way more important things to worry about than Nash.

At least that was how I thought before I saw him.

Nash lay on his back, a significant slab of rock pinning him to the ground around his stomach. His face was smudged brown with dirt and his breathing was like a constant whisper.

"Hey Parker," Nash said with a pained smile. The pain vanished when he saw Tes, and his smile was wide. "Tes! I'm so glad you're safe."

All of a sudden I could understand why Tes liked him. He seemed genuinely happy to see her. Unlike her father, he actually did care.

Tes blushed a little. "Me too," she said. The contents of my stomach rose in my throat. And I thought the meatloaf was bad going down.

Nash's eyes met mine briefly, but he looked away instantly and shook his head.

"Good to see you too, ya jerk," I said.

He looked at me again, but not with the anger I thought he'd have, but with pain—like he was actually sorry for what he'd done.

Then again, it could've just been the fact that he had a two-ton slab of rock nearly crushing his body into jerk-pizza.

"Hey Mickey. I'm glad you're safe, too."

Mickey. Normally the sound of that stupid name from this stupid brute would send my blood pressure into the stratosphere, but something in the soft way he said it made it sound less like a put-down and more like an in-joke between friends.

"Parker and I have been talking. I'm sorry for all the crap I've done to you. I just didn't want you to win after the challenge was already over."

Strangely enough, if Nash'd succeeded and I never got out of that broken capsule, I never would've brought Wesley to Kat. He inadvertently almost saved the world. That still didn't let him off the hook, though. It's not like he knew he was actually doing anything helpful.

"You're just saying that so I'll help you outta there," I said, half-believing my own pessimism.

He chuckled, or maybe whimpered, it was hard to tell. "No offense, Mick, but you're not exactly Mr. Muscle. It'll take more than you got to help me out."

Tes giggled. "He's got something way better than muscles." She nodded towards me.

"Why should I help him after all he's done to me? I don't understand why everyone wants to help him so badly. How do you know he's not gonna take my stuff and drop me in a hole somewhere?" I asked.

"You must be kidding," Parker said. "We gotta get him out! We can't just leave him stuck down here. He's in a lot of danger. He'll never get out of here himself."

Nash's eyebrows rose. "Is it true? Can you actually help me?"

The slab on top of Nash was large, but it shouldn't be a problem with the glove. There *was* a big problem though—the slab wasn't all that was above Nash. There was a stone pillar that rested on the slab.

"I can help," I said. "But it's dangerous. If we move that stone, the ceiling will destabilize. We could all get trapped."

"What are you suggesting we do?" Tes asked. "Just let him die?"

"I'm not suggesting anything. I'm just stating facts," I said.

Tes moved towards me, as if about to attack. "If you don't want to help, I will."

I backed away and shouted, "No way! I won't let you. It's too risky."

Tears swelled in Tes' eyes. She ground her teeth, rushed forward and knocked me to the ground. My head shot against the hard ground, rattling my brain and casting a brief blanket of stars in front of my vision.

Tes pulled at the glove. "Stop being a jerk!"

I sat up and rubbed the back of my head. The glove was no longer in my hand.

Before I knew it I felt her hand digging in my pocket. I pushed back, but she'd gotten the light-pen as well.

I stood up, but my vision went sparkly black all over again and I fell to my knees before I could stop her.

Then I saw the most frightening sight I'd witnessed to that moment—Tes pulling the stone away from Nash.

Dirt clouds shot down from the ceiling along with tiny rocks and clots of earth. Crumbling and cracking sounds echoed in the small cave.

Nash crawled out and pushed himself up. "Parker, get us out of here!"

"Right, follow me, hurry!" Parker yelled.

Stones the size of bowling balls crashed into the ground around us. And that was just the prelude. The pillar that had rested on the now-removed stone began to topple over like a baseball tee hit too hard.

A boulder slammed into the ground just in front of Parker. He leapt back, falling into Nash.

"There's no time to get out that way," I shouted. "Tes. Parker. Come over here."

They all ran to me, including Nash.

"There's a cove over there," I said, pointing. "It's too small for all of us." I removed my jacket and tossed it on the ground, in the shadow of the toppling pillar. "Nash, crouch down right where my jacket is."

I grabbed Parker and Tes and shot towards the cove. "Whatever, you do," I yelled to Nash, "Don't move off of that jacket!"

Tes turned to Nash. She must've seen the pillar falling towards him. "Gage, it's going to fall right on him!" She shouted, "Nash, get out of the—"

I pulled her arm down so that her ear was close to my face. "Don't tell him anything. You've got to trust me." I released her, and we made it into the cove. "Cover your faces. It's going to get really dusty."

Nash's face was alive with confusion and fear.

"Keep crouching!" I yelled. "Don't move."

"He's a sitting duck," Parker said. "We've got room here."

Parker was wrong. It was wishful thinking. There was barely extra room for a butterfly, let alone a gorilla-sized teenager.

"Just trus—"

CRASH!

The three of us huddled so close I was sure I'd lose all circulation in my body. After the initial assault of the ceiling on the floor, the wave of dust and debris made it painful to open my eyes.

So I didn't.

Tes did, though, and she screamed though the pain, "Nash! Are you okay?"

She broke away from us, but I grabbed her arm before she could escape.

"Wait for the dust to settle. You could fall through a pit," I said.

"Nash! Are you there?" Parker yelled out.

"Is it over?" Nash's voice sounded through the cloud of dirt.

We were silent a moment. It seemed like everything that was coming down came down. We emerged from the cove. Nash's silhouette crouched in place—he hadn't moved an inch. The column hung just inches over him.

Tes grabbed me and shook me with happiness. "How'd you know he'd be safe there?"

For me it was easy. The pillar's trajectory was set to collide on top of a large slab of rock that would hit the ground moments before it, creating a sort of bridge, and luckily for Nash, a kind of umbrella that would shield him from other debris.

"Lucky guess," I said.

"The bigger question is can we get back out?" Parker asked.

"It shouldn't be too hard," I said. "We may have to use the glove to move some rocks to make a stairway." I turned to Tes. "May I have it back, now? I need to find Dr. Renner and fast."

She caught me by the arm and activated the glove. The sensation was excruciating—kind of like having a million tiny needles pulling all the atoms out your body. My body oscillated from hot to cold every split second, and then, as soon as it started it was over.

I lay on the rocky floor, shivering and clenching my fists. "What was that for?" I yelled.

"You know I could hear everything you and Parker said coming down the pit?"

I froze in utter embarrassment. I wanted to crawl back in the pit and never make eye contact with Tes again.

"But that's not the only reason. It's also for not helping Nash the moment we found him. Don't ever pull a stunt like that again."

CHAPTER 16

DOG WHISTLE

"She's made of light?" Nash asked.

Describing what'd happened to me in the last twenty-four hours really made me understand the alienation Wesley must've felt trying to explain what was going on. Except for him it was worse—he'd been experimented on and mind controlled too.

"She's from an eon before the dawn of our time," I said. "Their people had a greater understanding of the world than we do. I'm not sure that she's 'made of light,' but she appears in the form of light," I said, fully aware that Nash must've thought I'd been beaten on my head with the crazy stick one too many times.

"That's awesome!" Parker said. "I can't wait to see her."

"It's actually very scary," Tes said. "She's got some kind of pin she sticks in your neck that makes you go crazy."

Parker rubbed the back of his neck. "I'll skip that part, but I'd still like to see her."

"The pin makes you crazy?" Nash asked. "What do you mean?"

Tes grabbed Nash and shook him. "Your body kinda does that, and then you seem to lose all ability to think for yourself."

I nodded. "Crane looked like he he'd been electrocuted. Then he came after us, trying to jab those things in our necks too."

"Maybe this guy just had mental problems," Nash said.

"Don't be stupid," I said. "It happened to Wesley too. Kat's controlling them somehow. She makes them lose control."

"Wesley's been doing that for a while," Nash said. "He's just a weirdo."

I replied, "Can you just stop making fun of peo—"

Tes put her hand on my shoulder, cutting me off. "No, no. It's true. He'd do it every time you blew that dog whistle."

Nash laughed. "Yeah, you remember the time I did it when he was drinking chocolate milk? He was so crazed he shot it out of his nose like a cartoon bull!"

Tes stopped and stared at him.

Nash's smile reversed instantly.

Tes snapped her fingers. "That's it. The whistle made him go berserk just like he did in the cave…"

Nash shook his head, and honestly, I felt his confusion.

Tes' eyes were wide, like she'd just discovered some great revelation. "It all triggers by sound…the pins manipulate their brains somehow with sound waves."

"Maybe that's why he wanted his earbuds so badly," I said.

"Earbuds?" Parker asked. "What's that matter?"

"He kept asking for them when we were going to the cave," I said.

Tes rolled up her slacks, showing a purple bruise the size of a baseball on her leg. "He even attacked me to get them."

"But what was making the noise in the first place?" Nash asked.

Tes' expression went blank and she stared off into nothing, then rolled her pants back down.

"It'd have to be something that can make high-pitched noise like a dog whistle," Parker said.

Tes nodded. "The metal in the cave! Maybe it vibrates ultrasonic waves, too."

"That's would explain why Crane didn't leave the cave," I said.

"Right," Tes said. "She wouldn't be able to control the sound waves without the metal."

It was actually a pretty sound theory, but there was still a problem. "But why'd Wesley go nuts in Dr. Renner's lab? There weren't any dog whistles or anything like that."

The confidence drained out of Tes' face. "I'm not sure..."

"Maybe it was Dr. Renner after all who triggered it," I said.

Tes shook her head. "Crane was watching him. He would have seen it. What happened right before he attacked you?"

I scratched my head. "I was trying to bargain with Dr. Renner. I told him I could show him how the glove worked, so I turned it on..."

The Rubik's cube clicked into place for both me and Tes. "The glove!" we said in unison.

"That ridiculous," Nash said. "What kind of glove makes noise?"

"Hate to say it," Parker said. "But I'm with Nash on this one. That doesn't make much sense."

I pulled the light-pen out of my pocket. "You're right. But it's not the glove, it's this."

"Looks like a laser pointer to me," Nash said.

I nodded. "That's what I thought, too. But look." I held it out. "There're two faders. One of them does shoot a beam of light, which changes color as you push the fader up."

"What about the other one?" Parker asked.

"I thought it was broken. But both have to be up to power the glove. I didn't get it until just now. The second fader must emit sound waves beyond our ability to hear."

"They're called ultrasonic waves," Tes added. "And they're what triggered Wesley's pin."

"And that's why we're going to capsule SC-14. Wesley must have hidden some kind of earbuds that help him to cancel out the effects of the sounds," I said.

"That could be a problem," Parker said.

"Why's that?" I asked.

He pointed to a capsule lying on its side on a hill of earth sloping down like a seesaw. "There's SC-13 but I don't see SC-14 anywhere. The Upheaval must've buried it."

"No way! Where is it?" I asked. "It's couldn't have gone too far."

"It's probably somewhere down there," Tes said, tiptoeing to the edge of a cliff and peaking down. "And it looks like we aren't the only ones looking for it." She knelt down next to a load-bearing peg with a rope tied to it. "It looks like someone's trying to get there first."

Chapter 17

Infiltration

"Maybe I should've stayed up there after all," Parker said, slipping off the rope onto the ground. "This place looks a little scary."

The hole was deeper than I'd thought at first. While much of the dust had settled, the smell of cool earth tickled my throat. The cavern was shaped something like the mouth of a wolf. The ground in the cavern was less like a floor and more like rocky teeth that jutted up and down. The earth over us also hung precariously. On the positive side, at least there were plenty of holes to let light in.

"Well, you're down here now, no sense going back," Tes said.

We'd decided someone needed to stay at the top to alert us if something happened. My vote was for Nash. I still wasn't comfortable with him. Both Tes and Parker had proved valuable to me in the past; Nash had been nothing but trouble.

"Don't worry about it Parker, Nash'll do a great job up there," I said.

"He would've done a great job down here, too," Tes said.

"Maybe," I said. "Let's fan out and find the capsule."

"Shouldn't we stay together?" Parker asked.

"It would be safer," Tes added.

"I don't know how long we have," I said. "And if there's someone down here, we need to find the capsule first. Tes, why don't you go south?"

Tes rolled her eyes. "Fine, whatever," she said, storming off to the north.

Parker looked at me and shrugged. "Guess *I'll* go that way," he said, departing southward.

That left me to go west. I crept forward, but the ground quivered beneath my feet. Maybe it really was for the best Nash wasn't down here. If the ground was crumbling under my small weight, it might not have been able to withstand someone the size of a small tractor.

I couldn't help but wonder why Tes was upset with me, though. I was just trying to do what was best to find the capsule so that I could save the stupid world. There was no reason for her to get all snippy.

A rock shifted under my foot and a hole opened up. I collapsed just to the side of the pit. Two things were certain. First, I needed to think less about Tes and more about where I was walking. And second, almost dying is a surefire way to get your heartrate up.

I pushed myself to my feet and took in a deep breath.

Before I could fully enjoy a calming exhale that would hopefully calm my nerves, a scream rebounded from the rocks seemingly from all directions.

I grasped my chest to make sure my heart didn't literally beat through. The good news was that it didn't, the bad news was that I recognized the voice—it was Tes.

I turned and dashed north.

"Help!" Tes' cry echoed through the cave.

"What's wrong?" I yelled.

"I'm coming," Parker's voice came from afar.

I knew it was stupid, but I really wanted to beat Parker there. I sped up, but slipped on another shaky rock. "Be careful!" I shouted. "The floor's very unstable."

Tes squeaked out a scared "eeeaaahhh!"

I shot up and dashed even faster than before. Over a jagged rock I saw her—well, I saw her fingers.

Parker emerged just beyond her, separated by a newly created pit. His eyes widened. "She's gonna fall," he said.

I dashed forward and slid, grabbing onto her hand. I crouched and tried to hoist her up, but I couldn't find a stable place for my feet.

"You're not strong enough," Tes said.

I finally found a foothold and pulled with all my might. Once again, however, I failed. Tes was right. I wasn't strong enough. I wished I were built like Nash, but I was just little me.

"Parker, hurry up. We need you," I said.

He crept carefully around the chasm.

The ground groaned underneath my weight. Waiting for Parker would take too much time.

"Hold on," I said, letting go of her hand. I pulled on the glove.

"Don't you dare," Tes said, eyebrows hardening.

"I have to. It's the only way," I said.

"I can hold on. Wait for Parker."

"There's no time," I energized the glove.

"Touch me and I'll rip your stup—"

I grabbed her arm and lifted her over the edge.

After moving to a more secure area, I powered down the glove.

Tes' face was red, her fists were clenched, and she glared at me.

"I had to do wha—"

Pain erupted on the side of my face. Tes slapped it so hard it felt like she'd been training to be a boxer for years.

"Hey! What was that for?" I asked, holding my hand to my cheek.

"For being a jerk," she said.

That was the second time she'd called me a jerk in the last twenty-four hours, and like hitting a thumb with a hammer in the same place, this time it hurt a lot more.

I backed away from my assailant. "All I did was help you. Why're you so mad?"

"I never asked for your help. Nash should've been down here to help me."

"We needed someone up there to watch out," I said.

"It could've been you, ya know. Or Parker...or me."

"What's it matter? We chose Nash to stay up there," I said.

"No, *you* chose him."

Heat coursing through my veins. "He volunteered."

Tes shook her head and her teeth glared as she spoke. "No, you just told him to stay, so he did. He was being cooperative, unlike you."

Parker arrived and stood between us. "What's up guys? You okay, Tes?"

Tes brushed her hair behind her ear and mumbled, "Yeah, I'm okay."

That's right. She was okay. So what was the big deal? I wasn't being cooperative? Because I didn't wait for Parker to get there? What was I supposed to do, watch her grip on the rocks slip and have her fall into a pit?

"Good," said Parker, nodding. He rubbed his hands, while avoiding eye contact with either of us. "I've got some good news. I found a capsule beyond this chasm."

"What? That's great," I said.

"Was anyone there?" Tes asked.

Parker shook his head. "I didn't get a close look before I heard you scream. But from what I saw, there wasn't anyone around."

"Are you sure it's Wesley's?" I asked.

"Not quite, but it's in the right area," Parker said. "We should at least check it out."

We rounded the edge of the chasm. The ground shook and shifted under out feet. I couldn't help but feel the same way about the tension between Tes and myself. If I said something, it'd be like the ground falling out between us.

Still, the silence between us felt weird too. I didn't want to say anything because I was sure it'd just make her angrier, but at the same time I wanted to make sure things were okay. I ended up saying nothing.

Tes cracked her knuckles and kissed them. They bled a little from some scrapes.

Parker held out his hand to look at them. "So what happened?"

"I just tripped on some really shaky rocks. When I fell, they just rolled down and took me with them. I was pretty lucky to be able to grab the cliff."

I was thankful for that, too. But I couldn't help but notice there was no mention of being lucky I was there to pull her to safety.

"Geez, we'll have to be extra careful," Parker said.

Tes nodded and wrapped her knuckles in gauze.

The capsule nestled against a stone wall. Parker was right, there were no signs of life, which made the rope hanging down all the more strange. Who left it there? More importantly, why?

"SC-14, we found it!" Parker said, holding his hand over his head for a high five.

I slapped it so hard my hand hurt as badly as my face had when Tes slapped me.

Parker turned and Tes hugged him. When they parted, Parker stepped aside for Tes and I to high five or hug, or whatever other way we would celebrate.

Tes brushed her hair behind her ear and I just stood there. Neither of us filled the distance left by Parker.

"So…" Parker started. "Anyone want to bet on whether the earbuds are in there or not?"

Tes approached the closed door and slammed it with her fist. "Why is this thing closed?"

I stepped forward. "It's no big deal, is it? Can't we just open it?"

"Oh my God!" Tes announced. "I just remembered. Wesley had special access from my dad. We won't be able to get in his capsule."

Parker nestled up next to Tes. "Is level 4 clearance special enough?"

Parker ran a card over the scanner and the door opened.

Tes' mouth hung open. "Where did you…"

"I, uh…found this card," Parker said with a chuckle.

"Make sure you keep your wallet close at all times when Parker's around," I said, climbing into the capsule behind Tes.

"I'll stay out here and keep watch," Parker said. "Five bucks says those earbuds are long gone. Any takers?"

"You're on," I said. "Let's face it, if I lose, I'm going to have much bigger problems than losing five dollars." The inside of the capsule was a maze of triangular bars, securing the integrity of the capsule against heavy external abuse. It also made it difficult to find anything.

"He may have secured the earbuds to one of the bars," Tes said, climbing into the capsule.

"Go ahead and check those, I'll look inside the sleeping chamber," I said.

I pushed the button and the lid slid off. I wasn't prepared for what was inside. When I saw there was someone in the chamber, I jumped back and banged my head.

"Someone's in there!" The words shot out of my mouth.

"Wha…who?" Tes asked.

I rubbed the back of my head. "It's Mr. Russell, Crane's partner."

Mr. Russell didn't stir from the chamber.

"Is he…" Tes started.

I stepped closer. "Dead? I don't know."

I peered inside the chamber. My rapid heartbeat was almost audible in the silence.

Mr. Russell lay on his side. There was color in his face, which was probably a good sign. I tapped his shoulder.

He groaned and moved a little.

"He's okay," I said, blowing a huge breath out.

"Ugh…says you…" Mr. Russell stammered. He sat up, holding his head. Looks like I wasn't the only one to sustain a bang to the head.

"Are you okay? What happened to you?" Tes asked.

Mr. Russell nodded with a grunt. "Who're you?"

"I'm Tesla Renner."

"Dr. Renner's daughter?"

"Yes," Tes said. "Have you seen him?"

Mr. Russell gnashed his teeth. "Yeah, I saw him. He's the one that knocked me out."

Tes covered her mouth. "Why'd he do that?"

"He came here looking for something. He didn't quite know what he was looking for, something that a kid named Wesley stole."

Crap. Dr. Renner got here before we did. It seemed that Mr. Russell was out of the loop though. Wesley didn't steal the earbuds, he created them. But how did Dr. Renner know about them?

"Did he find them?" I asked.

"Them? What do you mean? Did that Wesley kid steal a bunch of things?"

"He didn't steal anything," I said. "He made some earbuds that he needed to complete a mission."

Mr. Russell inspected his pockets. Alarm came upon his face. He looked around and patted down his jacket. "He stole them!"

"What?" I asked. "He took the earbuds?"

Mr. Russell sighed and shook his head. "No, I have the stupid earbuds. He stole the notes."

"Notes? What notes?" Tes asked. "What's going on?"

Mr. Russell's face flushed and he pushed passed me. "Can we get some fresh air? I'm getting a little claustrophobic."

Outside the capsule, Parker was flipping a coin.

"You again?" Mr. Russell asked, looking at Parker, who pocketed his coin. "What's going on here?"

"I'd love to explain," I said, "but can you tell us about the notes Dr. Renner stole first?"

Mr. Russell sat down and nodded his head. "I don't know. It's all pretty bizarre. The kid who wrote them sounded like he'd gone nuts."

"What do you mean?" I asked.

"It was like he was writing a confession. He was talking about how he'd been working for Dr. Renner even though he hated the guy."

"Nothing new there," Tes said. "Wesley didn't exactly hide his emotions that well."

"He said he was going to get back at Dr. Renner as soon as his 'mission' was completed."

I could guess what his mission was before Mr. Russell said anything. Wesley had a plan to go and destroy Kat and end the Upheavals. Of course Kat tricked me into screwing it all up.

"What mission?" Parker asked.

"He said he was going to stop the creature from waking up, end the Upheavals, and silence the voice in his head. If that's not the definition of crazy, I'll need a new dictionary," Mr. Russell said.

"He might be a little strange," I said. "But it's all true. Now your partner's in the same situation."

Mr. Russell crossed his arms. "Crane? What are you talking abou—"

Distant yelling from above interrupted our conversation.

"What's that?" Mr. Russell asked.

Tes dashed forward and inclined her ear. "It's Nash. We gotta go."

Parker and I pulled Mr. Russell to his feet. "You okay to walk with us?"

"I'll try," he said.

"Be very careful. The ground's really shaky here."

We hobbled off towards the rope. Nash was halfway down the rope by the time we got to the bottom, and it looked like he wasn't alone.

I shouted to Nash, "What's going on?"

"There's a guy coming after me!" Nash answered.

"Is it my dad?" Tes asked.

I stepped back to look beyond Nash. I couldn't believe what I was seeing. "It's Crane! He made it out of the cave."

"Is that good or bad news?" Tes asked.

"It should be good," I said. "Wesley was alright when he was outside the cave…generally speaking."

Nash released the rope and crunched onto the ground next to us. "Don't just stand there! He's after us."

Parker pointed up at Crane. "What's that around his neck?"

It was kind of like a necklace, except it was made of multiples pieces of thick metal. It wouldn't win any fashion points, but I doubt that was the purpose anyway.

"It looks like Barrix," I said. "Kat's using it to activate the pin in his neck."

"What the heck does that mean?" Mr. Russell asked.

"It means Nash's right. We gotta run," I said.

"This place is nothing but a dead end. There's nowhere to go," Parker said.

"Except up that rope," Nash said.

Crane released his grip and landed at the bottom of the rope with a *thud*. His face was red and sweaty, but it was the pins in his hand that I was concerned about.

"I've got an idea," Parker said. "Distract him and I'll steal the metal off his neck. Without that he'll be normal, right?"

I nodded. "Tes, get back. Parker and I will take care of this."

Nash jumped in front of Tes and pushed her behind him. He may've been a bully to me, but I had to admit I admired the way he protected Tes.

I took a deep breath and dashed forward. "Crane, can you hear me."

I think he nodded a little, but still held a pin out, ready to stick me.

"Crane, you need to fight her," I said.

Parker was inching to the side, out of Crane's view.

I flanked the other direction, doing my best to pull away Crane's attention. I was now close enough to see the pain in his eyes. His arms twitched and sweat dripped from him hair. He may have been putting up a fight, but it wouldn't last.

Like a leopard, he pounced at me.

I leapt to the side and crashed to the ground. The good news was that Crane had missed me by an inch. The bad news was that I had fallen to avoid the impact and was in no position to evade further attacks. I rolled on the ground, but Crane crash-landed on my chest, immobilizing me even further.

"Parker…" I stammered, coughing. "Now'd be…a good time…" I grabbed Crane's arms and tried to push, but he was too heavy and strong. "…to help…"

Crane grabbed my head and forced it to the side. The smell of sweaty hands and dirt rushed into my nose as rocks scraped the side of my face.

I knew he was going for my neck. I squirmed, but it was as useless as a fly struggling in a spider's web.

And just like that, I was free.

Crane's body vanished from off the top of me and he was now tussling with Parker. True to his skill, Parker had snatched the necklace, but it was still close enough to resonate.

I rubbed my face and pushed myself to my feet. "Throw it here."

Crane was too close for Parker to pass the metal off. Nash bolted over and tackled Crane. Unfortunately, he tackled him onto Parker. Parker crumbled to the ground with a heavy *thud*. The impact flung the metal from his hand.

Parker cried out in agony. Crane was on top of him, but to make it worse, Nash was on top of Crane.

Crane pushed off the ground like he was doing a pushup and flung Nash off the back of him.

"Gage, use the glove," Tes yelled.

The glove! "Great idea," I said, pulling it on.

Crane stood over the metal and hesitated a brief moment, as though it were a quarter he'd found under a urinal. His reluctance vanished in a split-second and he retrieved the metal.

Parker still lay bent over on the ground, coughing. He must've gotten the wind knocked out of him.

Nash backed off, going back to defending Tes.

I energized the glove and charged at Crane. At the very least, I could grab and incapacitate him long enough for everyone to get away. I swiped at him, but he dodged and pushed me to the ground, face-first.

Mr. Russell's voice came distantly behind me. "Crane, what the hell are you doing?"

That was the last thing I heard before I felt it—it was like having a shot, except that it was in my neck...and the needle moved up inside my skin and attached itself to my brain. But that was nothing compared to the pain that started to flood in after. Although I couldn't hear it, the burning felt like it was coming from my ears.

"Earbuds!" I yelled out. Then I heard *her* voice inside my mind.

{Come back to the cave,} Kat said.

{What? Get out of my mind,} I answered.

Pressure filled my ears, as if I were rocketed a thousand miles in the sky. Then, fire. Fire in my nerves. It flew like lightning tensing each muscle. If I didn't pee my pants right there, it surely wouldn't be long before I did, because I felt my control over my body leaving me.

I yelled, "Okay!"

The fire eased through my body.

{Now come to me,} Kat said.

I stood. Her voice echoed in my mind. I could barely even think my own thoughts.

{Leave now,} she said.

The rope was the only thing I cared about. Everything else blurred in my vision and I took off for it.

I grabbed it and started to pull, but then I stopped. I thought I smelled something pleasant, but couldn't place it.

Something changed—her voice was distant now, as if I was hearing it from under water.

{Don't stop!} Kat ordered. *{Or do you need more convincing?}*

Then the fire coursed through my veins again, but it wasn't like before. It was more like the hot sun on sunburnt skin, annoyingly painful, but not mind-bending.

Apples! That's what the smell was.

Tes' hands were on my ears. They felt cool against the burning sensation. Inside, she'd placed Wesley's earbuds. I turned to see her. Her dark eyes were frightened.

I smiled to let her know that I wasn't going to attack. Her face relaxed and she kissed my cheek.

{Come here, now!} Kat ordered, but it only a whisper now.

{No! I'm going to help my friends,} I answered.

But it turned out they didn't really need my help. Mr. Russell had thrown his partner to the ground. Between him and Nash, it'd be tough for Crane, even controlled by Kat, to do much harm.

Crane shot up, changed his aim, and charged for Tes and me.

I darted in front of Tes and anchored myself for impact.

Crane crashed into me and sent me flailing back, falling onto Tes.

Crane jumped and climbed the rope with amazing speed for an older guy.

{Don't even try to stop me, or they'll both die,} Kat whispered.

Kat was leveraging her control over Wesley and Crane by using them as hostages, but I couldn't let that stop me. I shook my head. *{Shut up.}*

I pulled Tes to her feet.

Nash and Mr. Russell checked on Parker. He was awake, but he was really out of it. He held his head and choked on his breath.

"What do we do now?" Tes asked.

"We gotta find your dad," I said. "He's got what Wesley made to stop Kat."

"What the heck happened to Crane?" Mr. Russell asked.

"Same thing that just happened to me," I said, rubbing the back of my neck. "Those pins are mind-control devices. Luckily for me, Tes put the earbuds in. It minimizes her control."

"Whose control?" Mr. Russell asked.

I told him about Kat and what Tes and I saw happen to Crane.

Mr. Russell shook his head. "I thought that Wesley kid was just crazy! That was all in his notes."

"What did he say?" Tes asked.

"There was a lot. Honestly, I didn't get all the way through. It all just sounded like a raving lunatic to me. The part I was most interested in was how he wanted to get back at Dr. Renner."

"What? How?" Tes asked.

"He said Dr. Renner was trying to use him to get out of the Junkyard, and didn't care at all about what happened to him."

Tes crossed her arms. "That does sound like Dad."

"But why'd he take the notes?" I asked.

"The notes explain his whole plan," Mr. Russell said. "You don't think he's going to try to destroy Kat himself, do you?"

"Not a chance," I said. "Wesley said Dr. Renner had no idea what was going on. He probably just thought his notes had information on some Relic."

"Dad was suspicious of Wesley. He knew he was hiding something," Tes said.

"That's probably why he took the notes," Mr. Russell said. "To find out what Wesley was hiding."

"Well, we gotta go find him," I said. "If he finds the cave, he's gonna give our only weapon to Kat."

Thud!

"What was that?" Nash asked.

I dashed towards the sound, and my heart sank when I saw what it was. "I've got some bad news. Crane cut the rope."

CHAPTER 18

KAT AND MOUSE

I didn't want to be the one who did it.

I enjoyed not feeling the fire in my body. But with no way out of the cavern, we'd have to use the glove to move some stones to make a stairway. I gave the glove to Tes and walked away. I wanted to be as far away as possible from the ultrasonic waves it took to activate the glove.

I checked on Parker. He was still pretty rattled. He found it hard to catch his breath or walk, but was certain he'd shake it off sooner or later.

I sauntered away towards the most distant part of the cavern as I could. I could immediately tell when Tes turned on the glove. I felt an irritating warmth under my skin.

And I could still hear Kat, whispering echoes in my head.

{It's no use fighting. I'm growing stronger every moment,} she said.

{Then why waste your time talking to me?}

{Because I like you.}

{You have a funny way of showing it, sticking this thing in my neck.}

{It's only bad if you don't obey.}

She sounded just like my parents. Everything I did had to be controlled, *for my own good*, of course. Well, at least I'd shown them. I made my own decision *for my own good.*

Unfortunately it got me in the situation with a pin in my brain. All I'd have to do is defeat Kat, though, and it'd all be okay. Sure, I'd never want to be near dog whistles again, but that wasn't exactly one of my favorite activities anyway.

{I'd prefer not to obey, thank you. I don't really like the idea of being a slave,} I said.

{You wouldn't have to,} Kat said. *{With me you can gain the power to change things.}*

{Is that what you told Wesley? Is that why he's got a pin in his neck, too?}

{Don't talk to me about Wesley. He's not like us,} she said.

{Like us? What do you mean? I'm nothing like you.}

Laughter ricocheted in my head. *{The mirror says otherwise.}*

Was she talking about the Relic that Nash had found? How did she know anything about that? *{What mirror?}*

{Don't play dumb,} she said. *{You really have no idea how far my knowledge extends do you?}*

{Why don't you tell me, then?}

{My link with the creature allows me to see what it sees, to know what it knows.}

{And what do you see?}

{That you're a mouse, just like I was.}

Kat was a mouse? *{I guess I would've thought of you as a different animal.}*

{You see, we really are the same deep down,} Kat said.

{So what? It's just a stupid mirror. What does it matter what animal it shows you as?}

{The mirror shows things closer to reality than your own eyes. Remember, you were dreamed up by the creature. It knows you deeper than you know yourself.}

{Okay,} I said, happy that the voice was getting quieter and quieter as I walked away from the group. *{And what does it mean that I'm a mouse?}*

{Like a mouse, and like me, you're destined to be experimented on. Don't you feel like you've been used by others for their own purposes? You're a lab rat. That is how the creature understands your meaning in the world.}

Fire burned inside my veins, but it wasn't because of her. The truth was that was how I'd always felt.

But now I knew better. I had broken free. I'd made my own choices. *{You're wrong,}* I said. *{Maybe that's who I was, but not anymore.}*

{Don't take it personally. That's how I was, too. But now I'm in control. And if there's one thing I know, it's that you don't have the power to be free. Not unless you...} Her voice was so faint I barely could make it out. I was near the end of the cavern now, next to a pillar of stone that made up the wall. I ran my fingers on its rough surface. It felt like sandpaper.

A deep vertical crack ran from the bottom as far up as I could see. But something grabbed my attention. Something white was caught in the crack, just above my eye level.

I pinched my fingers around it and pulled it out.

It was an envelope, bent and ripped a bit. It had a name on it—Dr. Renner's.

Could it be? Was it the letter I'd lost when I first got here? I flipped it over and ripped it open. Inside were some forms with my name on them. One was Mr. Brown-suit's evaluation of me, but behind it was a form I thought I'd seen before. It was the parental consent form that I'd forged to get here in the first place. But this one wasn't the same. It had my parent's actual signatures on it.

They'd known all along. Mr. Brown-suit went behind my back. He knew I was lying the whole time.

I crushed it tight in my hand and a small notecard fell from the stack of forms.

I collapsed on my butt and retrieved it. It was in my father's handwriting:

We understand that our son forged our names. He has never consulted us about joining the USDS [United States Delving Service], but after some time pondering the issue, we've decided to give our approval to his admission. Gage is a bright boy who needs the challenge and discipline we believe the USDS can offer. Thank you for notifying us.

I dropped the notecard. I wanted to light it on fire and stomp it into the ground. My nose was heated and if I'd had a pillow to punch, I would've beaten every last feather out of it.

Everything Kat'd said had been right. I wasn't the one who broke free. I was only here because of my parents. They were in control the whole time and could still pull me out of here if they wanted to.

"Gage," Tes' distant voice cut in the dusty air. "Let's go."

I threw the rest of the forms behind me.

Maybe I was a mouse, destined to be experimented on and controlled, but I was still determined to prove that I was in control of my own destiny.

CHAPTER 19

SPLINTER

We'd climbed out of the cavern with a clear mission—find Dr. Renner. We were down to three in number. Parker was still having trouble walking. So was Mr. Russell. Together they stumbled along okay, and Mr. Russell decided to take care of Parker and find a couple of capsules just in case an Upheaval was to erupt.

"So, you can hear her talking to you?" Tes asked.

"Only when the pin in my neck is being triggered," I said. "Luckily these earbuds do a good job muting the pain."

"If they're so useful, why didn't Wesley have them on him all the time?" Nash asked.

"Maybe he didn't want bullies beating him up and taking them," I said.

"The more important question is how do we find my dad?" Tes asked.

"Does he know where the cave is?" Nash asked.

"It's all in Wesley's notes," I said. "He's probably headed that way already."

"How do you know he's not there now?" Nash asked.

"Kat would've mentioned it, I think," I said. "Anyway, it doesn't matter, if he's there, we've pretty much lost anyway. We have to keep going as if he isn't there yet."

Tes nodded. "But where do we look?"

"We need to set up a perimeter around the cave," I said. "We'll have to split up."

Tes shook her head. "That sounds dangerous. What if someone falls or needs help?"

"I know it goes against the safety rules, but do you have any better ideas?" I asked.

Tes crossed her arms. "I guess not."

"I'll cover near the entrance to the cave. You two should cover the north and south sides around it, too. If he's not there yet, that's where we'll need to be present."

Nash stepped forward. "And what if Crane is still out there waiting for us?"

"I don't think we have a choice. If we stay as a group, we'll never find Dr. Renner. Are you in or out?" I asked.

Nash and Tes shared a glance and nodded.

"Be careful," I said. "We'll meet in an hour at the entrance."

That was the plan I thought would give us the best chance. I hadn't counted on the fact that one of us wouldn't make it back.

Chapter 20

Bargain

He was trapped when I found him.

Rocks were scattered all around Dr. Renner. The ground beneath him must've crumbled under his weight. He had fallen through the earth and rested in a huge rocky grave.

I knelt down at the edge of the pit. "Isn't that why we travel in groups? What happened to rule number one?"

He looked up and shook his head. "And where's your group?"

"Looking for you. You took something that belongs to Wesley."

"Just lower me a rope," Dr. Renner said.

"What's in it for me?" I asked.

He clenched his fists. "What do you want?"

"I want what you took from the lab. I want what Wesley'd been working on."

He laughed. "Not a chance."

"I'm not finished yet. I want the notes you stole from Mr. Russell, too."

His smile evaporated. "How do you know about that?"

"We found him knocked unconscious in Wesley's capsule. He told us you stole the notes from him."

"Get me out of here, already," he said.

"Do we have a deal?"

"There's no time. An Upheaval could happen any second. Are you really going to let me die here?"

"You're really going to lecture me about right and wrong after knocking out Mr. Russell and stealing from him?"

Dr. Renner's face turned red as a stoplight. "At least I had the decency to stuff him in a capsule afterward. You can't leave me down here."

"It's your decision, not mine," I said, and stepped back from the pit. Dr. Renner wouldn't be able to see me anymore, and I hoped that would help to make up his mind faster. But something ate at me. This really was a life and death situation. I couldn't just leave him down there, could I? What would Tes think?

I hovered over the pit again. "Well?"

Dr. Renner gritted his teeth. "Go throw yourself in a pit."

CHAPTER 21

CONTROL

Tes tapped her foot and glanced at her watch for the third time in the same minute.

"Where is he?" she asked.

She meant Nash, who was ten minutes late for our rendezvous time.

"We shouldn't have split up," Tes said.

"We had to," I said. "Just like we have to go now."

Tes adjusted the watch on her arm. "But what if he comes looking for us?"

"We'll come back once we get the device from your dad. Nash'll hang around here, I'm sure." Honestly, that probably wasn't true. It was more likely he got stuck somewhere like Dr. Renner had, or that Crane had got to him with a pin. But standing around here certainly wasn't going to help anything.

Tes scanned the terrain around us, probably hoping Nash would just show up unexpectedly. "I hope you're right. How far away's my dad?"

"Not too far," I said, placing my hand on her back and guiding her forward. "Come on."

Tes checked her watch a lot as we walked. I tried to distract her mind by talking to her, but she was too preoccupied.

Before long I was standing over the pit again.

"He's in there," I said, motioning to the hole.

"Oh my God! Dad! Are you okay?"

"Tesla!" He smiled. "It's so great to see you. Throw me a rope."

"No," I said, pushing her away from the pit. "Not until you give us the device Wesley was working on."

"I'm not giving you anything," he said. "You don't even know what it does."

"No problem," I said. "I'm sure Wesley wrote all about it in the notes you're going to give us as well."

Tes pulled me back and turned me to see her face-to-face. "Gage, we gotta let him out."

Tes being on her dad's side wasn't going to help. I mean, I understood why she was concerned, but I had to be stern here. It was the only way I'd be able to set things right.

"We can't just let him out," I said. "He won't just han—"

"Stop telling me what I can and can't do," Tes said. "You complain about your controlling parents all the time, but you're acting just like them."

Blood coursed in my veins. My face warmed and I'm sure it looked red with heat.

"You don't know the first thing about my parents," I said. "Besides, he's just trying to use you to get out of here."

Tes pounced and shoved me to the ground. "Shut up. If you won't help my dad, I will."

She pulled out her rope.

I lunged forward and caught her by the legs, tripping her. She banged into the rocks with a *thud*!

I crawled over her to swipe the rope from her hands.

UPHEAVAL

She grabbed my hair and with a painful yank, flung me off of her. "Gage, stop it. This isn't some stupid game. My dad's life is at stake."

I rubbed the top of my head, which still felt like it was on fire. Fighting Tes wasn't going to help my situation. I hated what I was about to do, but it was the only way.

"You're right," I said, picking up a rock. "Get a peg and I'll hammer it in."

She brushed her frazzled hair behind her ears, picked up the peg, and steadied it into a secure spot.

I banged it into place with the rock.

When the rope was secure, Tes threw it into the pit.

As she bent over to see her father, I pulled out my knife.

"I'm so proud of you Tesla," Dr. Renner said. "You've proven to be so resourceful."

I wanted to throw up at the sound of his shallow words. Tes looked like she was falling for all of it though. She smiled and I could've been mistaken, but I thought I saw a little water in her eyes.

He took hold and began to climb the rope.

"It's okay, Dad, we'll get out of here."

"I never should've doubted you," he said.

"Just a little more, then take my hand," Tes said.

That's all I needed to hear.

I pressed the knife against the rope. "Give the device and notes to Tes now," I said. "Or I'll cut this rope."

Tes' attention shot towards me. "Gage...don't you dare!"

"What's going on?" Dr. Renner asked.

"Do it now!" I said, sawing into the rope with the serrated knife.

Tes' eyes widened. If there wasn't before, there were definitely tears in her eyes now.

"Dad, give me the notes," she said, looking down at him.

"Are you kidding?" he asked.

"Just do it, please," she said, choking on her words.

I heard the rustling of paper and Tes bend down. She took them in her hand and threw them at me. The pages scattered like confetti and fell to the ground.

"I can't believe it," Dr. Renner said. "You were just manipulating me."

Tears fell from Tes' eyes. It wasn't a pretty sight, and it hurt me to do it too, but I still needed Wesley's device.

"One more thing," I shouted loud enough for Dr. Renner to hear. "Give Tes what Wesley was working on."

"Dad, it's not my fault. This wasn't what I wanted."

Tes turned to me with tears in her eyes. She wanted me to stop, and I really wanted to also, but I had to do this for the greater good.

"Do it," I said.

She bent down and took the machine in her hand.

"How could you do this to me?" Dr. Renner asked Tes.

Tes turned to me, holding the device. "Alright, you got what you wanted, you jerk. Now let him up."

Under any other circumstances I wouldn't hesitate to help him up. But if I did, he could overpower me. Tes would hate me for it, but I had to stop him. Hopefully she'd understand.

I shook my head. "I'm sorry."

I sawed through the rope. Tes dashed at me to stop me, but by the time she crashed into me, it was too late—I'd cut the rope.

The tail of the rope whipped past us and down the hole. Dr. Renner crashed onto the ground and gave an angry yell.

"He's okay," I said, pulling Tes' hands away from me. "He fell down once, it probably hurt, but he'll be fine. The important thing is to stop Kat from triggering any more Upheavals."

Tes' face was wet with tears and strands of her blond hair obscured parts of it, but her eyes scorched me with anger.

"I'll never help you again," she said, pushing herself up to her feet.

"I'm sorry, but I had to do it," I said, gathering the papers on the ground.

"And I'm sorry I have to do this," she said and kicked me to the ground. The good news was that it didn't hurt too badly. The bad news was that the ground shifted below me, then crumbled. I fell with the rocks twenty feet or so.

That hurt.

Tes yelled down to me. "I'm gonna save my dad myself since you sabotage everything I do."

The notes I'd collected glided down into the pit like fall leaves.

"You can't! You don't even know what you're doing," I said, regathering the separate pages.

There was no response.

She was gone.

Tes' anger had doomed us all. She had no idea what to do with that device. And since the papers were with me, she wouldn't have a chance figuring it out.

Things couldn't possibly have gotten worse...

Until I noticed I wasn't alone—I was sharing a pit with Dr. Renner.

CHAPTER 22

WESLEY'S NOTES

Dr. Renner and I had a pretty long rope, Wesley's notes, my glove and a knife. The one thing we didn't have, and that I desperately needed, was a bodyguard.

Dr. Renner limped towards me. I must've busted his leg when I dropped him down the pit that last time. I'd have felt worse about it, but he shambled after me like a zombie. I'm sure he had worse things in store for me than eating my brains, but I wasn't going to just sit there and wait.

I shot up and felt an immediate bolt of pain travel up my thigh. I hopped away against the rocky wall. Our quarters were about as big as a living room, which was far too small for evasive maneuvers to be successful.

"Where is it?" he asked, grabbing me by the collar. His breath smelled like a lizard's early morning fart.

"Where's what?" I asked.

"The device."

"Tes took it."

He clenched his fists and groaned. "Idiot!" he said and shoved me to the ground.

Like father, like daughter.

"You have no idea what you've done," he said. He staggered over and picked up some of the papers.

"I know exactly what I was doing. I was going to use to stop the Upheavals."

He handed me the papers. "And do you know exactly how you were going to do that?"

I smoothed out the crumbled notes. "I was going to use Wesley's device."

Dr. Renner just nodded. "Go ahead and read how he planned to do it."

Wesley's handwriting was predictably terrible, like a second-grader's writing during an earthquake. But what the notes had to say was far worse than his handwriting.

Wesley's device was built on the same technology used to upload Kat's consciousness into the metal. Wesley reconfigured the device to do the opposite—to remove Kat's consciousness from the computer. It sounded good, but I delivered Wesley right to her, and now Tes would be heading into a trap with the only weapon we had.

"How much of this did you know before you read this?" I asked.

"I didn't even know if it was real until now."

"And how'd you figure that out?" I asked.

"I ran into that guy who ransacked my lab."

"You mean Crane?" I asked.

"He was wearing some kind of metal around his neck. He seemed just as out-of-his-mind as Wesley sometimes got. He attacked me and I ended up getting knocked into this pit."

"I don't understand, what does that have to do with the creature in the earth?"

"It's all in Wesley's notes. The metal, the pins, the creature. I thought he was crazy until all this happened."

"He's not crazy at all. I've seen it myself. Tes and I were trying to destroy the computer that was built to keep the creature asleep."

"And now, because of you, my daughter is going to try and destroy the computer, which means she'll probably end up with one of those pins in her neck as well."

Dr. Renner painted the situation pretty dark, but I knew that to win any game, you had to keep positive and watch for any opportunities.

The good news was...um...

I tapped my fingers on my legs.

Good news...

Crap! It was all bad news.

CHAPTER 23

A NEW PLAN

So apparently Kat wasn't always a computer program. According to Wesley's notes, she was actually a regular girl at one time. In an earlier eon, she was chosen by her parents to be the one to keep the creature in the earth asleep.

At first she was reluctant, knowing that the job meant she'd have to give up her physical form and be computerized in some way. But she didn't really have much of a choice in the matter.

People from that time used the pit to gather energy from the creature. It was all experimental stuff, but eventually she was connected with a pin in the back of her head. That was just the first step.

At least now I knew where she got *that* idea.

All that remains of her physical body now is the form of light that she reveals in the cave.

What puzzled me the most was how Wesley knew any of this. Kat never told me about any of this. She must've told Wesley, but why would she even mention any of it to him in the first place?

Dr. Renner sat on the ground across from me, staring at the rope on the ground and scratching his head. While he was trying to figure out how to get out of the pit, I was busy contemplating Kat's motives.

I pulled out the light-pen and turned on the sound fader.

Heated pressure pulsed in my ears and through my body. It was annoying, but thanks to the earbuds, not completely mind-bending.

Kat's whisper manifested in my brain. *{There you are. I've been waiting for you.}*

{I've got some bad news for you,} I thought. *{Wesley's built a weapon to destroy you.}*

{It's only too bad he can't use it. He's with me right now. He's put up a good fight, but he's helping me quite well now.}

{He might not be able to use it, but I certainly can.}

{I don't think so. I know your secrets. You're destined to be used and manipulated, just like I was.}

{Are you talking about how your parents made you sacrifice yourself to become a computer?}

For a moment, I heard nothing in my mind. I wondered if I'd scared her off.

{Who told you that?} she asked.

{Wesley did, and I was wondering how he knew. You must've told him yourself.}

{Don't worry about him. He's nothing but hands to me now.}

{Then why'd you tell him about what your parents did to you? Is he your friend?}

{It doesn't matter now. He turned out to be just like the rest of them.}

{Like the rest of who?}

{Everyone.}

She must've been talking about the people of her eon—the ones that died when she awakened the creature.

{Is that why you killed them?} I asked.

{You know better than anyone. They were just using me so they could keep their lives the way they were. People don't want to do what's hard, so they make other people do it for them. Isn't that why Dr. Renner has you all here in the first place? The people of my time destroyed my future by connecting me to a machine, and for what? Well the jokes on them, because it's their futures that are gone and I'm the only one left.}

{Is that what you're going to do to us, too?}

{Soon enough.}

{But why?}

{You really haven't been listening. Because you're all like them. Even Wesley...}

{Wesley? What'd he do anyway?}

There was another silent moment.

{So this weapon...you have it now?}

{Yes,} I lied.

{And how is it supposed to work? My information is stored in the Barrix. It's as indestructible as the creature itself.}

That may have been true, and Wesley's notes confirmed it, but there was still a weakness. She told me that the metal can exhaust and have to recharge. It may not be a solution, but was at least a weakness I could try to exploit.

{Then I guess you have nothing to be afraid of,} I said and slid the fader off.

Dr. Renner had the rope slung around the pillar in the center of the pit. He held the ends and tried to use it to climb, but it was still too steep. He collapsed to the ground with a grunt.

He pushed himself up and kicked a rock. "If only there was a better place to tie this rope."

He was right about that. There really wasn't any good place to tie the rope to climb up. The pillar near the center was a column—kind of like a tree with no branches. It was also the primary structure that kept what was left of the ceiling from collapsing down. Dr. Renner and I had already broken two significant holes in that structure.

It did give me an idea though.

"I know what to do," I said, pulling on my glove. "But it's dangerous."

He picked up the rope and coiled it in his arm. "Whatever you have planned is going to be less dangerous than sitting down here waiting to get killed in an Upheaval."

"Maybe," I said. "We'll see about that after I do it."

"Okay. What do you want me to do?"

I charged the glove and felt the familiar heat course through my body. "Stand under the hole," I said. "The roof is going to collapse."

I wasn't sure how the glove would respond to such a heavy load, but I didn't really have any better ideas, either.

I grabbed the column and pushed.

It didn't move. Pretty bad time for the thing to stop working.

Dr. Renner shook his head. "You never should've cut the rope."

"It's not like you've been super hel—"

CRACK!

The column cracked just above where I'd been grabbing it. The cracks traversed the pillar horizontally until they met around the other side.

The lower quarter of the boulder flickered in and out of space thanks to the glove.

"Stand still. You'll be safe there," I yelled. "But cover your head."

Of course it was like a lobster in the pot yelling to its friends in the aquarium to keep safe. *I* was the one who was in danger.

I pulled the boulder free and the rest of the pillar hovered above the ground, still connected to the ceiling.

With another loud crack, the top of the pillar broke free and tumbled down. The good news was that the pillar was taller than the pit was wide—it would crash and come to rest on the wall at about a sixty degree angle. The bad news was the ceiling that it'd been holding up was no longer being held up.

Hands grabbed my shoulders and flung me away. I ended up on the rocks with Dr. Renner lurched over me. Plumes of dust rose as rocky shrapnel flung everywhere.

When the dust settled, I coughed quite a bit, which was good news—it meant I was still alive and breathing. Dr. Renner coughed as well.

"You okay?" I asked.

"Yeah," he grumbled. "You were right about this spot." He motioned with his hand around us. Stones the size of basketballs and slabs like bricks littered the landscape all around us. Above us was nothing but sky.

I nodded. "That pillar held quite a load, huh?"

He grunted in approval, still working the dust out of his lungs. "How'd you know it would work?" he asked.

I supposed he was talking about the rest of the pillar. It was still mostly intact and now lay against the wall of the pit like a stairwell. The only way it'd be easier to get out of here was if the pillar had actual steps on it.

"I just have a knack for spatial comprehension," I said. "Chess, Rubik's cubes, mazes, it all just makes sense to me."

He patted down his pants and shirt, sending out tiny plumes of dust. "Well, you sure did a pretty good job on this one."

"Except for almost crushing myself under a ton of rocks."

Dr. Renner held his hand out to me. "Safety rule #1, always travel with a partner. They can help save your life."

Normally, I wouldn't have trusted him. In fact, this whole time I'd been pretty sure he was trying to stop me, or at the very least was making my life harder on accident. Wesley said Dr. Renner had no idea what was going on. But he risked his life to save me from the falling rocks. Not to mention he didn't throttle me the second I fell down the pit—the same pit I'd refused to save him from, then trapped him in all over again.

Needless to say, I was a little ashamed and a lot confused.

"Why are you trying to help me?" I asked.

"You've read Wesley's papers. If it's true, we're in a lot of trouble."

"Do you believe him now?"

"Does it really matter?" he asked.

"Of course it matters," I said. "If it's true, the whole world could be coming to an end."

"Right," he said. "And if he's wrong, he's obviously got some amazing Relic down there. Either way, it's something I need to be there for."

Tes was right about one thing—her dad really did want to get out of the Junkyard. Even with the threat of worldwide destruction looming, he still was thinking about finding something that would get him out of here.

I couldn't help but laugh.

"What's so funny?" he asked.

"I was thinking the same way when I first went in that cave."

"And now?"

I shook my head. Now?

Now I was concerned with the one thing Dr. Renner should've been—Tes. If Kat didn't buy my lie about having the weapon, the danger she would be in would be quadrupled.

Hopefully Kat would be looking for me, not her.

Unfortunately, I didn't really know how powerful the pin in my brain was. I didn't know that Kat already knew that I was lying.

CHAPTER 24

ROADBLOCK

Kat wasn't lying about one thing—she really was getting more powerful. That was really bad for two reasons: her control on people's minds would no doubt strengthen, but even more pressing was what was happening as a side effect…

The sirens blared in warning.

She'd agitated the creature…another Upheaval.

We'd escaped the pit and were well on our way to the cave, but we'd never make it before the ground beneath us shifted.

We sprinted at the siren's warning. Dr. Renner did his best to keep up, but his legs were pretty sore from two falls down a pit, no thanks to me.

"We need to find a capsule," Dr. Renner yelled.

The earth rumbled and cracked beneath our feet.

"No way," I said. "I'm going for the cave."

"We'll never make it."

"Then find a capsule," I said. "I have to try."

"Are you sure?"

I really wasn't, but I couldn't help but think of Tes. She was out here somewhere, and she had the device. With her dad beside me now, I couldn't believe how much of a jerk I'd been. I never should've used her like I did.

I *had* to save her. I'd never forgive myself if I didn't.

"I've got no choice," I said.

A pillar of rock shot up in front of us. I grabbed Dr. Renner and pulled him around the obstacle.

"Come with me. I'll leave you at the first capsule we can find."

"Just don't throw me down another hole," he panted.

I pulled on the glove. I didn't like the idea of having Kat in my head again, but the glove could give me some extra help.

I turned it on and the pressure and heat was greater than I'd felt before, even with the earbuds.

The earth shivered under our feet like thin ice under heavy weight.

"Ease right," I said, pulling Dr. Renner with me.

The ground beside us crumbled into stones and toppled down a freshly exposed chasm.

"How'd you know that wou—"

I knew he'd wonder how I knew that and frankly so did I, but I also knew something much more terrifying would happen beneath our feet currently.

Before Dr. Renner could finish his sentence, the ground vaulted down beneath us. It was less like an elevator and more like a slide—one with no guard rails, plenty of pits, and hard rocks to smash up against. If it was a ride at Disney World and I knew I'd live to see the end, I'd probably do it again though.

We bounced on our butts and back to our feet a couple times.

{I see you're still alive,} Kat said.

{I guess you've gotten what you need from Wesley.}

Dr. Renner and I grasped onto each other. The mutual support at least allowed us to do most of the downhill on our feet, even if it was more like hopping down a hill than running.

"You're not going to like this part," I said. "But just go with it and you'll be okay."

His head swiveled at me, but I continued to watch the rolling earth around me. If I had to guess, I'd imagine his eyes had an expression that said, *oh great, now what?*

I shoved him as hard as I could. We repelled away from each other like billiard balls.

A large pillar of stone crashed into the earth right where we would've been.

{You're not going to stop me,} Kat whispered.

That's what she thought.

Dr. Renner tumbled and came to rest on a small platform.

I ran to him and helped him down.

"You're not going to like the next part," he said, echoing me.

"What do you mea—"

He punched my arm. "But just go with it," he said.

It hurt, but I did drop him twenty feet down a pit. We'll call it even.

"What now?" Dr. Renner asked. His eyes shot all over.

"Take a deep breath," I said, and pulled him an inch to his left, next to me.

The ground around our toes crumbled and we plummeted about two stories.

The rocks we landed on hurt way worse than a punch to the arm, but it was the boulder that was falling straight towards us that scared me the most.

"Holy—" Dr. Renner shouted before covering his head.

Then, it stopped.

The Upheaval stopped.

So did the boulder, which I held right over my head, thanks to the help of the glove.

Dr. Renner uncovered his face. The look in his eyes said, *I'm alive?*

"If you still need it, there's a capsule about twenty feet from here," I said.

Dr. Renner nodded. "Look, I know you said you were good at understanding spatial-three-dimensional stuff, but *come on*. It's like you knew what was going to happen."

I hadn't really thought of it, myself, but he was right. This Upheaval was different. I tossed the boulder on the ground away from us.

{*Impressive, little mouse, but I've got what you want.*} Kat said. The thin scent of apples surfaced in my memory.

{*You haven't seen anything yet. I'm coming to get you,*} I thought.

Dr. Renner pushed himself to his feet and patted my shoulder. "After this is all over, we could really use you, you know? That was amazing. The USDS could really put your skills to work."

Kat laughed. {*Don't let him butter you up too much. Remember, lab rat, that's all you'll ever be to them. They will use you until they get what* they *want. I'm sure you'd make a great ticket out of the Junkyard for him.*}

My face heated, and it wasn't because I'd just avoided death. She really knew how to get me angry.

"Shut up," I said, throwing my hands down.

Dr. Renner stumbled back. "What?"

I turn away from Dr. Renner. {*Leave me alone,*}I thought. I shook my head and turned off the glove.

"Sorry," I said. "I didn't mean…"

Dr. Renner moved in front of me.

"You okay?" he asked.

"I'm fine. Let's just find Tes."

Dr. Renner looked around. "Oh no…"

We were deep inside the ground again. Overhead was mostly sealed off by earth, but this time it wasn't a sealed pit. It was more like a cavern.

The good news was that I knew exactly where we were. The bad news was that I didn't like how I knew exactly where we were.

I had felt something when I turned off the glove. The heat coursing through my veins went down, sure, but I felt something in my mind go off.

"Her connection to the creature is going to be enormous," I said.

Dr. Renner faced me. "How do you know that?"

"Because I felt my own connection to the creature through the pin in the back of my neck. That must've been how I knew what was happening during the Upheaval."

"That's a good thing, right?"

I shook my head. Not for Tes. Kat knew where she was, and she was playing with me about it.

"We gotta go now," I said.

CHAPTER 25

REGROUP

Inside the cave, everything was just as I'd feared.

We were too late.

The corridor was dark and quiet.

Nash rushed out of a hidden cove to warn us. "They've taken Tes."

"What do you mean?" Dr. Renner asked. "Taken her where?"

"They put one of those things in her neck."

Heat coursed in my face and arms and cool sweat dripped down the side of my chest. "Why'd you let that happen?"

"It's not my fault," Nash said.

He was right. It was really my fault for pushing her away. But I didn't want to admit that, especially not to Nash.

"Then whose fault is it?" Dr. Renner asked.

"Look, I tried to stop him," Nash said. "But he was too fast for me."

"What? The guy's like a million years old," I said. "You couldn't stop him?"

Nash's head tilted slightly. "What?"

"Crane, the old guy," I said.

He *was* old, but I knew from earlier that he was still very strong, especially under the control of Kat. I was just angry because I wasn't there to help her.

Nash shook his head. "No, it wasn't him. It was Fido."

"Wesley?" Dr. Renner and I said in unison.

That made even less sense. Wesley had the body type of a couch potato. Nash had the body type of Tarzan. "How'd Wesley get the better of you?" I asked.

Nash crossed his arms. "I'm sorry, I was really sore and out of breath."

"Where'd this all happen?" Dr. Renner asked.

"Just inside the cave. He came out of nowhere."

What? Why was Wesley leaving Kat's room? He was the one she needed to do work on the core.

"Did you see Crane anywhere?" I asked.

Nash nodded. "That's why I was late to our meetup. It's also why I was so sore and out of breath. I ran into him while I was looking for Dr. Renner. He nearly stuck one of those things in my neck, but I took care of that."

"How?" I asked.

Nash smiled. "Old tricks, Mick. I locked him in the broken capsule."

I shook my head. Honestly, I was just glad I wasn't the one he was shoving into that thing.

"Nash! I'm impressed," Dr. Renner said.

Nash eyes lit up. If I had to guess, it was the first compliment Dr. Renner ever paid to the guy.

The celebration was short lived though, as the current situation shadowed over him. Nash shook his head and frowned.

"We still have a real problem, though. She's got Fido and Tes in there now."

"So there are two of them and three of us," Dr. Renner said. "Sound like we've got pretty good odds."

If numbers were all that mattered, I'd say we had good odds. Unfortunately, just like in chess, every piece is worth a certain number, and three pawns were just not better than two rooks, knights, bishops, or any combination of them. The real problem was that we had no weapon.

Unless...

"Nash, did Tes have anything with her when she got taken?"

Nash nodded. "Yeah, she had some kind of machine. She said she could use it to fight Kat."

"Do you know what happened to it?" I asked.

He nodded. "Fido took it."

I shook my head.

"What do we do now?" Dr. Renner asked.

"We have to get it back," I said.

CHAPTER 26

TRANSCEND

The cave was alive with cool vibrations. Dr. Renner, Nash, and I stalked around the sides of the cave. As we neared Kat's hideaway, the fire coursed through my veins. It was more intense than usual, even with the earbuds. But there was much more to worry about. I was most afraid of having to fight against Tes. She'd be controlled by Kat, but I really didn't want to have to hurt her.

I also was afraid that she'd be the one hurting me.

{Guess who I found?} Kat asked.

The scent of apples came to my mind again. She was somehow manipulating my brain to smell things.

{Leave her alone,} I thought.

{It's too late for that. But don't worry, she's embraced it pretty quickly.}

The scent got stronger. Was Kat doing that to me to make me mad? It was weird. I somehow knew where Tes and Wesley were. It was the same as when I knew what was going to happen during the Upheaval.

{Do you know where I am?} I asked.

{I see you and your two companions very clearly.}

Wesley mentioned that Kat started her union with the creature by using one of these pins. Were we now partially sharing our mind? Was that what made us able to communicate?

Kat spoke, *{There's no use hiding, come on in here.}*

I motioned for Nash and Dr. Renner to walk in the entrance. "She knows we're here."

"How does she know?" Dr. Renner asked.

"Either the information coded in the sound waves flying around, or through the pin in my neck. I'm not sure which."

"What's the plan?" Nash asked.

"I'll try to distract her," I whispered.

{You can't distract me, little mouse. I'm everywhere.}

"Find the device and see if it still works," I said.

{Oh it works, just not the way you think.} Kat said.

Dr. Renner and Nash nodded, and ducked into the entrance.

I followed, sure of only one thing—we were dismally outmatched, but even a lowly pawn can become the most powerful piece in chess if allowed the opportunity. We just had to play towards that possibility.

Inside was Kat, illuminated in the middle of the room. Next to her were Wesley and Tes. They both looked terrible. Their hair was like they'd just awoken from a four-year nap and sweat covered their faces. Tes, who was usually stunning even covered in dirt, looked ill and tired.

Wesley closed a lid on his device. How terrible for him. Somewhere inside his mind, he must know that he was holding the very weapon he created to fight Kat, but couldn't find the resolve to use it.

"Let them go," I said. "Can't you see that you're killing them?"

"Why should I care? If I didn't do this, they would have no problem trying to kill me."

Dr. Renner and Nash crept around the room on either side. Tes and Wesley watched their every movement.

"Nobody'd want to hurt you if you weren't trying to control them," I said.

"That's not true," she said. "When I was a child I wasn't trying to do anything, but my parents still sacrificed me in order to keep the creature from destroying them."

"That was them. We're not like them," I said.

"You're all like them. Everyone is."

"You don't really believe that," I said.

"And why shouldn't I? Name one person who doesn't try to control others," Kat said.

"What about Wesley?" I asked. "You let him go. You let your guard down for him. You must've seen something in him."

Kat crossed her arms and shook her head.

"Why'd you let him go?" I asked.

The ceiling and walls illuminated brighter.

"I *thought* he was different. I *thought* for a moment he really was what the creature had been trying to create for so long."

"And what's that?" I asked.

{Nice try, trying to distract me.}

Wesley dropped the device and lunged at Dr. Renner. Tes did the same at Nash.

Wesley crashed into Dr. Renner. They both fell to the ground. Wesley removed a pin from his pocket and climbed onto Dr. Renner's back. Dr. Renner rolled to the side, repelling Wesley from on top of him.

Nash fared a little better. Even with the pin enhancing Tes' strength, Nash was too quick and flung her to the ground.

"Be careful," I yelled. "Watch their hands. The last thing we need is to get outnumbered."

My ear singed with heat.

{I can't tell you how mad it makes me that you won't listen to me,} Kat said.

The device lay on the ground completely unguarded. She must've wanted it this way. On the other hand, maybe this was the opportunity I needed.

I dashed forward and retrieved the device.

{And why should I listen to you?} I asked.

{Because no one gets to change their destiny,} Kat said. *{I was a mouse and my parents used me. You're the same, yet you constantly try to prove you're not.}*

{And why does that upset you so much?} I asked.

{No one ever gave me a chance to do things my way. But you won't listen to me. They're all trying to control you, but you go along with them anyway.}

{The only one trying to control me is you,} I said.

{You're wrong. You're here because people want to risk your *life to find* them *power. Dr. Renner's been doing it for years. He does it with his own daughter. And yet you continue to work for him.}*

{And that's what your parents did to you, isn't it? They forced you to connect with the creature, so they could stay alive.}

{Exactly. I never had the chance. But you do.}

{And what choice am I supposed to make?} I asked.

{Become like me. You don't have to be a lab rat for them. You can take control. No one will tell you where to go or not to go, what to think or feel. They won't risk your life for their glory. They can't.}

Kat was right about one thing—at times I really hated my parents for hovering over me. They always knew what I got on a test at school before I did, and there was hell to pay if it didn't meet their expectations. They were constantly checking my grades. They wouldn't let me hang out with friends without interviewing them and making sure they were "good for me." I couldn't listen to music without their permission. I couldn't even eat without them making sure it was "good for me." Why the hell did they get to decide *everything* that was "good for me?"

Hot blood sped through my arms and my heart beat faster. I was so tired of my life at home and so excited to come here. But Kat was right, and Wesley told me the same thing— the government was using me to get what they wanted. They were just as bad as my parents.

So was Dr. Renner. I hadn't seen him shed a single tear for his daughter. Not one. He just wanted to get out of here and he didn't care what the cost.

{And you're offering me a chance to have the same kind of power as you?} I asked.

{There's no reason not to,} she said. *{The creature has more energy than any one person could possibly exhaust. You and I could continue on together, watching each civilization come and go. Maybe with our help, we could help the creature sculpt a better world...one that can't be abused.}*

I had to admit, it all sounded pretty good. But something still bothered me. *{Could we take Tes too?}*

{Why would you want to allow her to be like us? She dropped you into a pit to die. She's not like us.}

Tes *did* kick me into a pit, but after what I had done to her, I really didn't blame her. *{That doesn't mean that I don't still like her.}*

{Like her?} Kat asked and laughed. *{She hates you.}*

No way. Tes didn't hate me. She was just mad. Okay, furious, but definitely not hate. And she only was so mad at me because I'd been a jerk. She was right. I'd been treating her like my parents treated me.

{Don't believe me? Become like me and you'll know.}

{I'll be able to read her mind?} I asked.

{Come and find out. Do it and you'll know.}

Her words thrust me back like a powerful gust of wind. *Do it.* I've heard that mantra a thousand times. I even said it to Tes myself.

And that's when it all clicked.

"I'd never want to become like you," I yelled. "All you want to do is control people."

"And why not?" she asked. "Isn't it better than being controlled? You forged your parents' names. You cut the rope. You say you don't want to be like me, but you already are."

"And every time I've done it, it's made me worse. It's not about who I am, it's about who I want to be. And I don't want to be like you or my parents."

"That's why you can never beat me," she said. "You're not willing to do what it takes to have true power."

"But I have this," I said, weighing the device in my hand. "This is what can destroy you."

"It's only too bad you can't use it. You know that I let you get it. And you know that I want you to use it."

"Why do you think you know so much about me?" I asked.

"Because I know you. I used to be just like you. We've been stepped on and controlled all our lives. You only have one choice in your life—you can be controlled or be the controller. I'm giving you the chance to be like me. Take it now. This is your last chance."

A loud thud of bodies crashing to the floor echoed behind me. I turned to see Tes anchor a pin in Nash's neck, who seemed to have been knocked out. I wouldn't have long.

"Before I choose, I have to ask one question. Why'd you let Wesley go? Is it because you loved him?"

The metal structure in the room shot down with a sudden heavy load of light, and it gave me an idea.

"What does that matter?" she asked.

"With a pin in his neck, there's only one way Wesley got out of here—you must've let your guard down. Is it because you loved him or not?"

"I'm not capable of love. My parents' stored my mind into metal. I'm more computer than human now. Besides, love is weakness. I am power."

"Then why'd you let him go?" I asked.

"He tricked me. He's a filthy liar."

"How could he lie to you if you could infiltrate his mind? What did you find there that made you let him go?"

The Barrix flickered like a lightning storm.

"No more questions. What is your decision?" she asked.

"I know you loved him. You say you have so much power, but could you make him love you?"

Light pulsed from the ceiling and walls. The heat in my body from the pin throbbed.

"You don't know anything about it," Kat said.

"He refused to be with you, and now you're trying to get me to be with you. That's why you want me to be like you, isn't it?"

The metal oscillated light, like a candle flickering before dying. Only, Kat didn't extinguish yet.

Kat thrust her arms behind her, like she was pushing back water. "Go ahead and use the weapon if you like. I already know you won't. You're too timid to become anything other than the lab rat you are. Your parents are right to control you. You need it. You have no mind of your own. Your destiny is only to kneel."

My hands tightened on the machine. She was playing the same game as I was, except that I was now impervious to her poison. But she didn't know that yet, which was a tactical advantage for me.

My attacks were certainly angering her, but not enough. The metal wasn't giving off enough energy to exhaust it.

The good news was that I now knew how to blind her with anger. The bad news was that I wasn't going to like it.

I dropped the device and maneuvered towards Wesley.

"You're right. I can't use this weapon. But it doesn't have to be my decision, either. Maybe I *am* a mouse. Maybe I have been used in the past. But the funny thing about mice is that they are more than just lab rats. They're also excellent maze runners and puzzle solvers. Everything's not about power. Some things are about being creative. And as for kneeling, sometimes you have to kneel in front of those you love."

I removed the earbuds and stuck them into Wesley' ears.

All the tension drained from his muscles.

I wish I could've said the same about mine. It was like I was thrust into a burning furnace. I knew I wouldn't be of much help now, but Wesley hopefully knew what I discovered—he was the one who Kat really cared about. He was the one who could appeal to whatever goodness was in her. And unfortunately for Kat, he was also the one who could upset her the most.

{Get Wesley now,} Kat ordered me.

I had no choice but to comply. I tried, but it was like she was sending lightning through my body, making it move like I was a puppet. Sweat precipitated on my forehead and chest. I was no longer in control.

I grabbed Wesley' hoodie and pulled him down. He rolled over me like a tire running over a curb. Tes dashed to us to help me restrain Wesley.

Dr. Renner rushed over and pulled me away from Wesley. I watched my legs kick and flail in the air as if I was nothing more than a marionette.

"It's over," Wesley said, taking the device and pushing himself up.

Tes tackled Wesley like she was sacking the quarterback in the last minute of the Super Bowl. He fumbled the device while Tes pushed his face to the side.

"Earbuds," Kat said. "Get them."

Tes clawed at Wesley' ears, but he punched back sending Tes to the ground.

Wesley rubbed his head and stood back up. "I've been waiting for this moment for a long time."

He picked up the device again.

"Do you have any idea what that machine will do?" Kat asked.

"Of course I do," Wesley said. "I built it. I built it to complete what you started. Isn't this exactly what you wanted all along?"

Kat's body illuminated so bright I had trouble looking directly at it. "Yes. But not like this," she said. Her voice sounded choked up. "You lied to me. You lied and you're a thief."

"You lied first," Wesley said. "You said you would keep the world safe from the creature. You said you wanted me to help."

"None of that was a lie. I wanted you to rule with me. I wanted you to dream a new life and a better world. I wanted someone to share it with."

"No one in their right mind would want to share anything with you. That's why you put that thing in my brain isn't it? Deep down you know that you'll always be alone unless you force someone to be here. That's why you let me go, isn't it? Even you didn't know. You had to see for yourself if I'd stay with you?"

The ceiling and walls were blinding. Nothing stood out against the pure white that flooded everywhere.

"You could've been all powerful," Kat screamed. "Just like me."

Then, with a sudden whoosh, the light dissipated. The fire in my body was gone as was the pressure in my ears. Best of all, there was no voice inside my head.

"What happened?" Tes asked, shaking her head.

"He did it!" I said.

Dr. Renner released me from his grip. "So now what? She's just gone?"

Wesley rushed over to the console in the middle of the room. "Not even close." He opened the console and withdrew a circular circuit. He tied it to the string around his neck. "She'll be back very soon, but her link to the creature will be unstable again."

"What does that mean?" Tes asked.

"She won't have as much control to wake up the creature. But she's not gone. The Barrix's gathering energy, then she'll be online again."

"But she'll be less powerful, right?" I asked.

"Yes, kind of. It might've been a mistake, but I had to get her upset long enough to dismantle her connection."

"Dismantle her connection? Why's that matter?" Dr. Renner asked.

"She won't be able to wake up the creature this way. But she'll still be able to control us."

"So we should get out of here before she comes back online?" I asked.

Wesley's fingers twitched around the circuit in his hands. "Probably not. She may have already done it—awakened the creature, that is. That last outburst was pretty loud."

The walls emanated a faint hum with a shimmer of light. Warmth coursed through my arms and legs. The Barrix was charging.

"I'm going to have to try to dismantle the core for good," Wesley said. "But Dr. Renner's the only one without a pin. He won't be able to protect me long enough."

"Give me the device," I said.

Wesley picked it up and held it to his chest. "Why? Do you know what this thing will do?"

"It'll connect my mind with the Barrix, like what happened with Kat."

Wesley nodded. "How'd you know that?"

"She told me," I said. "She's coming back online any second. One of us needs to battle her for control while you dismantle the core."

Dr. Renner moved towards Wesley. "That thing gives your mind access to the same power as Kat has?"

Wesley backed away. "Get away. It won't work on you anyway."

A bead of sweat ran down from my armpit. "Give it to me now, before it's too late."

"But you don't know what it means. There may be no way of coming back," Wesley said.

"He'll be trapped forever, like her?" Tes asked.

"Could be," Wesley said, nodding.

"Give it to me," Dr. Renner said.

Wesley pulled a chord from the machine. "It plugs into the pin," Wesley said. "You can't use it."

"I'll do it," Tes said, taking the device from Wesley.

"No! Tes, stop," I said

"You're not the boss of me, Gage," Tes said.

"Tes, I'm sorry for what I've done to you, but don't argue with me on this."

Tes fidgeted with the device, her eyes avoiding me. She hesitated, just as anyone would, probably because it may mean she'd never come back.

Kat's voice whispered into my warm ears, but it was too faint to understand.

"She coming back online," I said.

Dr. Renner's hand hovered over his daughter's shoulder. It seemed like he wanted to stop her, but he knew he couldn't use it on himself. Our eyes met and he nodded to me.

I nodded back.

Dr. Renner snatched the device from his daughter and tossed it to me.

"Gage!" Tes yelled.

{What are you doing?} Kat asked, as if from underwater.

I gritted my teeth and removed the chord from the device. I thrusted the needle into the pin in my neck. Heat ran from the back of my head all the way to my toes, and then, like falling asleep, I didn't feel anything anymore.

But I saw everything. It was like I was looking at the room from every angle at the same time. I watched my body collapse on the ground as if I'd fainted. Tes ran over to it and put her hands over my chest.

I could feel her fear, like ice being rubbed against warm skin.

Nash sat up and held his head.

Wesley was already busy working on the core.

"Gage," Tes said.

{I'm here,} I said.

She looked around the room as if expecting to see me.

{It's so nice to feel the presence of another here with me,} Kat said.

Kat may have liked it, but to me it felt like we were twins sharing a womb.

{You feel claustrophobic?} Kat asked.

I guess it was easy for her to tell. It was like we were having two thoughts in one mind.

{You know why I'm here?} I asked her.

{You think you can diminish my power, but I know something you don't yet understand.}

{And what's that?} I asked.

{Watch.}

The sound from the walls ascended to a high tone, only now I was able to hear it for the first time. Well, maybe not hear. It was more like a really pleasant vibration, warm and sweet.

For Tes, however, it meant excruciating pain from the pin. Her face contorted and she rushed after Wesley.

She grabbed his hood and threw him back.

This time I could help, though.

{Stop,} I said to Tes. *{Get away from him.}*

Tes hesitated, clenching her fists.

Dr. Renner came and pulled her away from Wesley. Wesley limped back to the core.

{You see what you've done?} Kat asked. *{You've controlled her.}*

{So what?} I asked.

Nash tackled Dr. Renner, freeing Tes from his clutches. She rushed after Wesley again.

{Tes, stop!} I said.

Tes came to a standstill.

{Isn't it wonderful?} Kat asked. *{You could make her to do whatever you want. You can make her be whatever makes you happy.}*

{That's not good enou—} I started.

{Get him now!} Kat said to Tes.

{No!} I said.

Tes twitched and bent over. Her face was red and her hands were clenched. The conflict in her mind seemed to be ripping her apart.

{What do you want her to be like, Gage?} Kat asked. *{Just tell her and she'll do it.}*

{You know that's not good enough,} I said.

199

{How do you know unless you try?} Kat asked.

{Because it wasn't good enough for you. That's why you let Wesley choose. And how'd that work out for you?}

"Keep it up, Gage," Wesley said, pulling a metal plate revealing circuits. "I think I can end this soon."

{Gage, if you won't do it for Tes, do it for the world. Think of it. Together we could build a world without suffering. The creature, with all its power, does nothing to solve the problems of the world. We could control it.}

Controlling the world to make it perfect sounded great. If I had created the world, my parents wouldn't have breathed down my neck every moment of my life. Jerks like Nash wouldn't push kids like Wesley around. It'd be so much better.

Except...

If I controlled it all, people wouldn't be free. I'd be just like my parents, telling everyone what they should do, "for their own good." Maybe it's worth it to have people being bad if it allows for people to be free.

{I'd rather have the creature sleeping and doing nothing than you controlling everyone for their own good.}

{But it won't just be me. You will be in control, too.}

{Control just isn't for me, I'm a mouse remember?}

Wesley pulled something out of the console and waved it in the air like a flag.

The good news was that when Wesley removed the circuit from the central console, all the lights went out.

The bad news was, so did my mind.

CHAPTER 27

AFTERMATH

When the lights came back on, I was on a metal table. Wesley and Tes grabbed my arms and pulled me up. Everything was shaky, like I'd just come off a roller coaster.

When I regained my focus, I noticed Wesley had a syringe aimed at my arm, ready to stab into me.

"What's your name?" Tes asked, squeezing my arms to my sides.

"Umm, Gage...why are you guys acting weird?" The room was grey and small. I think we were in the medical wing of campus. "Where's Parker? Is he okay?" I asked.

Tes' hands relaxed and she smiled and turned to Wesley. "I think that's Gage."

Wesley nodded and set the syringe on the table. He lifted up two fingers. "How many fingers am I holding up?"

"Of course I'm Gage, who else would I be?"

"We didn't know if we extracted you or Kat or both from the metal."

"What are you talking about? I'm me. That shouldn't be too confusing. Now where's Parker?"

"Oh, right," Tes said. "He's the next door down. He's fine."

"So the world didn't blow up or anything?" I asked.

Tes looked around the room. "Looks like we're all still here. That creature must be a deep sleeper."

"Well that's a relief," I said.

Wesley nodded. "For us, but it will wake up some day and start all over again."

"As long as no one tries to control it, I'm okay with that," I said.

Tes' hair was messy and her face was covered in dirt. I could only barely smell the apples.

"What's wrong?" she asked.

I guess she could see the disappointment on my face. "I know something that you don't want me to know."

"What do you mean?" Tes asked.

My head dipped a little and I looked at Wesley.

"I'll just see my way out," Wesley said, and closed the door behind him.

"When I was in the metal with Kat, I could see some things…"

Tes covered her mouth.

"I thought you were just really mad at me. But I could feel something in you. It wasn't just anger. You hated me."

Tes curled her hair around her fingers. "I did, but—"

"Look, I'm sorry for what I did with Nash, and your dad, and, well, just everything."

"Don't forget taking the device from me," she said, crossing her arms, half-smiling.

"First of all, I'm pretty sure *everything* covers that too. And to be fair, I didn't do that one because I was trying to be a jerk; I did that one because I didn't want you to die, or get trapped, or whatever I was afraid that thing was going to do to me."

Her smile was now full. "So, what else did you see in me?"

"I saw that you are a wolf, and that it means you value loyalty and being part of a group."

"Do you think the creature's dreams about us are set in stone? You're a mouse and I'm a wolf. Do you think we can change it? Do we get to create our own destiny?"

"Yes," I said.

She laughed. "Yes, what?"

"We are what we are. I'm like a mouse—clever, fast, and quick to figure out a good maze. As for destiny, the creature's asleep. Kat wanted to force everything to fit her will. The creature creates, but lets us be free. I like it better that way."

Tes nodded. "I wonder what happened to Kat, anyway."

So did I. If Tes and Wesley could get me out...

"How'd you guys bring me back anyway?" I asked.

Tes shook her head. "We didn't really do anything except pull the device out. I guess as long as your physical body was okay, that's where you mind in anchored."

"I think Kat's body is long gone," I said. "Maybe the Barrix is all the body she has left."

"So, you think she's trapped?" Tes asked.

"As long as the Barrix lasts."

"Isn't it indestructible?"

I nodded. "She was alone for so long. I think all she really wanted was love, but she could never admit it to herself."

"Why not?" Tes asked.

The door creaked open, and Dr. Renner entered.

"Sometimes the person you love doesn't notice, so it's easier to deny it," I said.

"You're awake!" Dr. Renner said, placing his hand on Tes' shoulder. "She's been here for hours you know, waiting for you to wake up."

"Dad…" Tes said, lowering her head.

"Is everyone else okay?" I asked Dr. Renner.

"Parker got hit pretty hard, but he'll be fine. Crane and Russell are both working hard talking to the USDS. Nash and I got a bit banged up in the fight, but everyone made it out okay."

Tes stepped back, leaving Dr. Renner's hand holding the air. "And what about me? You said I was manipulating you."

He sighed. "I know I've let you down, Tesla. You shouldn't have to pull me out of a pit for me to tell you how proud I am of you." He held out an open hand to her. "Forgive me?"

"It's not that easy," she said and scooted by him, leaving the room.

Dr. Renner ran his hand through his hair. "Do you think she'll ever come around?"

I nodded. "If I learned anything about Tes, it's that you have to earn her respect. She may not realize it now, but you did a lot to get it back when you took the device away from her."

Dr. Renner laughed, shaking his head. "She was pretty mad about that earlier. Her moods are as unpredictable as the Upheavals."

The Upheavals. Curiosity flooded my mind. Now that the core was dismantled, what would happen? "Are they over now, the Upheavals?" I asked.

Dr. Renner nodded. "It seems so. Data gathered from around the country indicate that seismic activity has returned to normal."

I know it seemed weird, and I should've been happy, but the news was kind of bittersweet. The worst part for me wouldn't be going home to my parents. I felt like I could live under their rules better now, especially knowing that even they wanted me to be here.

No, the worst part would be not getting to see Tes and Parker anymore. Even Nash and Wesley had grown on me a little. "So what happens now? Do I just go home?" I asked.

"While the Upheavals have stopped," Dr. Renner said, "we still have work to do. Crane, Russell, and I have discussed it and think we should have at least one more week to excavate. Who knows what we could find?"

"And that'll be okay with the higher ups?" I asked.

"This is the Junkyard. They won't care," he said.

"And if we find something great?" I asked. "Then what?"

"Then I get to put together a team for future projects," he said. "Are you in?"

If you enjoyed this book, please take the time to rate and review it on Amazon.com. To keep informed about upcoming books by Ryan J Slattery, join his mailing list by signing up at www.rjslattery.com.

ACKNOWLEDGEMENTS

Over a year's worth of work went into the creation of this book. In all that time a lot of pieces got lost in the mix and there were many people to help put the pieces back together.

I want to thank my children, who are always my inspiration and the primary audience I write for, even though they are far from reading the book at the date of publication.

I also want to thank my wife, Molly Slattery, who encourages me to continue to follow my heart, even if it means hours and hours in front of a computer screen.

I must thank my thoughtful beta-readers who notice and point out the aforementioned pieces out-of-place. They provided me with insight, encouragement, and just enough criticism to make the story work better. Thank you Tina Rak, Chanacee Ruth-Killgore, April Bergener, and of course the Red Inklings, particularly Steve Murphy and Ashley Ortiz.

Great gratitude must be expressed to those with the least enticing job—proofreading. Ryan Sextro, Pat Post, and Steve Murphy, Thank you for combing through a manuscript full of imperceptible missing "the's" and grammar errors. The most thankless job is also the most necessary and the book would be utterly unreadable without your efforts.

Lastly, thanks to those of my students who eagerly encouraged me and showed literal sadness when they learned the release date was months away. That kind of enthusiasm revitalizes me when the craft becomes drudgery.

About the Author

Ryan J Slattery is the author of imaginative middle grade and young adult novels. Upheaval is his second book. He lives in St. Louis with his wife and two children, teaches seventh grade, and will one day fulfill his destiny and create the ultimate breakfast hot-dog.

Made in the USA
Lexington, KY
11 May 2016